Is It So?

Edited by Peg Alford Pursell
Designed by Adam Robinson
Cover image art by Kevin McIlvoy

Library of Congress Control Number: 2023935557
McIlvoy Kevin.
Is it so?: glimpses, glyphs, & found novels / Kevin McIlvoy.
ISBN 978-1-7336619-3-5 (pbk) | 978-1-7336619-4-2 (epub)

Published by WTAW Press
PO Box 2825
Santa Rosa, CA 95405
www.wtawpress.org

WTAW Press is a not-for-profit literary press. We are grateful for the assistance we receive from individual donors, public arts agencies, and private foundations.

CALIFORNIA
ARTS COUNCIL
A STATE AGENCY

Glimpses, Glyphs,

& Found Novels

KEVIN McILVOY

WTAW Press
Santa Rosa, CA

Contents

Found Novels

From the Writer's Wife:
An Introduction to *Is It So?*

In the summer of 2022, Mc handed me the manuscript of *Is It So?: Glimpses, Glyphs & Found Novels* for comment. I read it with an accumulating sense of wonder and told him, when I'd finished, "Mc, you have written a quite marvelous *last book*." His response, typical of him—his habit of humility and his confidence in the power of truths left unspoken—was silence. A warm silence. Did I feel in that moment the cool shadow of foreboding of his death, less than four months away? I can't say that I did. That shadow had always been with us.

Death figures prominently in *Is It So?* but it was not for that reason I perceived culmination in the pages of this book. These pieces offer fulsome evidence of Mc's decades-long preoccupation with somatic prehension; with storytelling via indirection, transformation rather than transaction, and enacting rather imparting; and with the diction and rhythms of vernacular speech, especially what is withheld from or hidden inside speech. The stories in *Is It So?* demonstrate his deepening commitment—already so evident in *57 Octaves Below Middle C* and his two subsequent novels, *At the Gate of All Wonder* and *One Kind Favor*—to the irreal, the carnivalesque, to ghost stories, fairy tales, the short short form, and to prose poems or—in his words—writing that lands in "the gulley" between prose and poem. *Is It So?*, his final book of fiction, is also so much who Mc McIlvoy, the artist and the man, had come to be in the last decade of his life. A tremendously skilled "hybridist" (a term I borrow from Sebastian Matthews' essay on Mc's oeuvre, published in *Asheville Poetry Review*, Spring 2023), playfully mashing up literary genres with visual art and music. An evermore gentle spirit toward children and the inner child. A ruthlessly clear-eyed comic on ageing bodies and ageist erasure. An activist increasingly enraged by capitalism's destruction of beauty, human dignity, and democracy. And, within all that energy, a calm-abiding Buddhist dedicated to a practice of seeing, saying, and letting go.

The first six pieces in *Is It So?* can be read as Mc's instruction—subtle and indirect as ever—on how to read his work. In "A Difficulty" the narrator says, "I get goldfish, really get them. I can be them, draw them—still—and moving." The narrator in "If a small ocean" says that in his art he "render[s] the mass and the volume under the masks the body wears," and that he has "studied the techniques for drawing transparencies because clear surfaces found me in every subject appearing before me."

Mc is telling us that his lifelong compulsion to carefully listen to and observe people, their speech, and their circumstances—especially those who are odd, overlooked, or actively dismissed—has led him to perceive everywhere *story*, suggested but never completely, coherently exposed, and always expressed through the consciousness unique and subjective to that being and that circumstance. I'm indebted to Sebastian Matthews for succinctly articulating in his essay Mc's commitment to perspective in his fiction. Mc told stories, Matthews says, "from *inside* his characters, utterly from their point of view, inside their heads and hearts; thus, what comes off as whimsical or slightly mad or wildly surreal or just a little strange is actually true to life…the real-time lunacy of being human, of one human trying to connect with another."

These attempts to connect—in service of and despite the real-time lunacy of human heads and hearts—inform every piece in *Is It So?* In "Cake all day," which Mc told me was one of his favorite stories he ever wrote, a paralyzed, cognitively impaired stroke survivor and her brother-in-law pass their time during his visits to her "attentive to each other's self-talk," which centers on cake, object of desire and wonky, deflective metaphor for all the suffering neither can bear to address directly. Dorothy Eva and her visitor are a thought experiment in co-conscious connection: "They did not ask each other to clarify what they overheard...They did not interleave...They took turns witnessing, alert in the listening."

Even the most overtly political pieces in this collection, such as "Sharpied on a damaged MAGA car windshield," enact attempts to connect. The series beginning with "De-installation ceremony, Whitherton, North Carolina, May 18, 2019" features the tribal omniscience narration of the de-installation work crew performing a deep dive into the perspective of their most alien imaginable Other—a Lost Causer as broken by the assault on his worldview as the Confederate statues the workmen have dismembered and pissed on.

The "found novels" in *Is It So?* wed Mc-the-novelist's paradoxical fascination with the short short form to this book's focus on rendering transparencies. Set in Desordenada, North Carolina, a made-up town name suggesting disorganization, the novels Mc "found" there extend the concept of the found poem into a novel's worth of *suggested* story. The few words comprising each novel are the transparency that veils and evokes prehension of the withheld narrative. The terms "glimpses" and "glyphs" in the book's subtitle underline its fealty to radical compression and to rendering the mass and volume of what is only ever implied. A glyph is a symbol or pictograph, conveying more information than is visibly present. The glimpses offer a more complete narrative but shatter or torque it by unexpected shifts in time, perspective, or frame.

In "Passersby," Mc-the-hybridist joins his omnivorous appreciation of music with his late life venture into dance as another means of inhabiting music with his established habit of storytelling through the consciousnesses of the sidelined.

Here, the bit players with walk-by roles in Gene Kelly's famously virtuoso dance performance of "Singing in the Rain" in the 1952 film of the same name take center stage, to assert humbly yet passionately that their bit parts in a seminal event matter precisely because of the strenuous effort of their artistry to get it right.

"Blue Squill" begins as a story in third person about Mr. Jordan Jabbok, a retired dance instructor battling a flock of diabolically vengeful crows for control of his garden, but rapidly shifts frame to a first person dialogue between the writer of Mr. Jabbok's story and his sister, a nonwriter who hectors him endlessly about his inability to properly shape— and especially to end—a story. This writer-narrator, who is Mr. Jabbok's neighbor, says "my writing life had made me a devastated and undeterred gardener-gladiator…it has broken open more room in me for welcoming the magic hour and the magic object held forth as a projection of holy possibility in a world that has lost all sense of the sublime." In the next story in the collection, "Mr. Jabbok's story ends as you would expect"; his death and the scattering of his ashes in his garden allow the neighbor-writer-narrator to evoke his own probable ending: lost battles and a call for truce.

This book may be the most personal of Mc's prose works. In the autographical bits—disguised, as is all autobiography in all his works by veiling, distortion, and transposition—he is, as I see it, putting his heart in order. There is reckoning— the jettisoning of romantic notions about self and others, and acknowledgment that too often our self-delusions mean we fail to see what's beneath a clear surface. But there is equally present the hard-won wisdom of an elder taking the long view on life's trials and joys, and the inevitability of death. The forest ranger at the center of "In the Gila" chides the narrator, "You don't see what you should." But the outcome of their several uncomfortable encounters over decades is a release of the murky animus between them "all at once and for always."

Although this book tunnels deep into the dark and desperate recesses of long-life experience, it ultimately leads to light: in the final piece, a pilgrim in the DMV slowly ascends dusty stairwells to the Office of the Clerk of Happiness. Having observed Mc's self-directed transformation from contemplative Catholic to Buddhist embracing not religion but ontology, I read *Is It So?* as a writer's testament to walking the path with awareness, blessing equally what is and what is no more, moving incrementally further into joy by letting go of attachment, delusion, aversion—and life.

Christine Hale
June 2023

"The fantastic is that hesitation experienced by
a person who knows the laws of nature, confronting
an apparently supernatural event."

(TZVETAN TODOROV, *THE FANTASTIC*, TRANS., RICHARD HOWARD)

A difficulty

"No luck?" my wife said.

"The clear plastic bag is the problem."

"Hard to do."

"Impossible."

"The goldfish," she said. "A difficulty."

"Oh," I said, "I get goldfish, really get them. I can be them, draw them—still, and moving."

"Fantails?"

"God, yes. All their lives they look middle-aged, muddled."

"You're better at drawing the goldfish, then?"

"Better at everything, *at everything* I try to draw. Except for—"

I shook my head.

She shook hers.

In the slipstream of the sheets, we expectantly undulated.

"Some wine?" she asked.

"A sip. Thanks."

"Are human mouths still an issue?" she asked.

"And hands. Feet. And noses. I really hate the fuckin' noses on people."

She said, "A nose holds it all together."

"Noses shouldn't look like that," I said. "Should they look like that?"

If a small ocean

Having read my mind, my wife asked a rhetorical inebriated question, a dance of sound and light resisting shape as a sentence: "Do you have Magdalen the Bartolommeo drapery the drapery do you still have the her that you keep in the all your all of your notebooks?"

"Oh, her drapery," I said, because the gesture and the form of *The Magdalen* by Fra Bartolommeo pulled at me almost to the point of immobilizing me; *The Magdalen* is in every one of my notebooks.

I answered, "I would give my gallbladder for that kind of drawing magic. I *get* drapery. I can *be* drapery—do we have another bottle?" Inside, I was still fuming about the noses, about the fact that I could draw animal noses and tree protuberances and the grilles of Dodge Challengers and Olds Toronados and Studebaker Champions but not human noses, not for the life of me; and I could sometimes, very poorly, do that joining of shoulder and arm that does not easily come forward in a drawing except with the most skillful attention to edge light; and I could do mouths, though even a slightly open mouth with teeth and with the shadow evidence of a palate and tongue made me panic.

I looked into her wineglass for a vantage point.

Glancing at the wriggling likeness of my eyebrows and temples on the liquid surface, she thoughtfully avoided mentioning my buttocks-drawing period from which I never fully recovered. A little bit more sloshed, she said, "How people wear the people drapery—I'm glad I don't haven't won't draw them."

I did not say what I was thinking. That there should be Drawing Viagra, the smallest dose causing such swelling excitement that a simple chalk sketch of calf viscera could throb with tactile, after-death expressions of weight. I was thinking that Restore Apps should jolt the memory centers that help in drawing the tension-revealing shapes and not the mere lines of emergent forms. I was thinking that the Greek artists—the pantheon of the greats!—failed utterly at anatomical accuracy; that I was too old for the unending apprenticeship of the artist who wants to get drapery right, to render the mass and the volume under the masks the body wears, to show sunlight and wind dressed in the clothes pinned on the line and dancing, to draw the veiling and unveiling processes inherent in every manifestation of filling and flowing and flooding.

She knew I would not give in. If a small ocean must be carried from here to there, I do not rest from the task. I summon the transatlantic steerage space of my immigrant grandmother with her bulging valise, with her splintering bloodshot eyes gazing into the wasting faces of her children and her parents.

On the 6:25 a.m. Tunnel Rd E1-427

Slouching in sunrise concavity, the stranger reveals that she is Mildred Maneless-Gastaing, her tone suggesting I should recognize her. By way of apology, I say, "Something is terribly wrong with my memory," and, rather lamely, I ask, "Pets?"

She holds them before her. "My beauties." I feel her looking at me through the clear plastic bag, fixing her concentration on my face and, in particular, my nose. I explain that for two decades I studied the techniques for drawing transparencies because clear surfaces found me in every subject appearing before me. My anathemas come to meet me—more unrelentingly than ever, they find me everywhere. If I pass children in a playground, one will always have in hand a bubble-blowing wand. If I ask my boss at the bowling lanes for overtime pay, she removes her smeary glasses to avoid hear-seeing me. If I'm hiking alone, barely visible drapes of spiderweb windows appear. If I'm dreaming of sexual intercourse, thigh-high, clear vinyl boots will vice-press my neck. If asking Mr. Tchelitchew the price for a fifty-sheet book of tracing paper, his unkind voice roils his vape fumes.

I tell Woman on Bus about Van Gogh and my wife and Chaim Soutine. Vincent Van Gogh sold one painting, one painting in his whole life.

"Is that how it goes?" This was the thing Van Gogh said to himself more or less constantly. So loud that people could hear: "Is that how it goes?"

Van Gogh was astoundingly productive between 1880 and 1890, and that was it, really, because fear ruled all his other years.

I tell Woman on Bus about the problem of her and her shape-shifting goldfish, that she and her clear plastic bag are a reminder that I will never meet a fellow passenger who does not inspire horror.

"Not much oxygen in the bag," I say.

She says, "Very little."

"You've come a long way with them?"

"A great distance."

"And you are transporting your fish at 6:25 a.m." They are in a bag that is beautiful. Inexpressibly beautiful.

"I am. Transporting them."

When the bag settles again on her lap, the interpenetration of bus light and first light on her skin and on the bag-skin and on the scales and stressed crimson gills of the fish and on the windows and the not-quite-dull aluminum window frames, all of it causes me to wish I could have permission to sketch her nude, to render the intersection of her body with the bus's hard surfaces, the event of her skin and the world's vulnerable skin touching for that moment, which is something I could get and could be.

"Lively," I say.

"We are. And bright, don't you agree?"

Wineglass

The newly uncorked wine my wife offered was red wine splashed into the mouth of a simple clear glass with a clear stem, with the music of the spheres in its recurved rim.

The ways in which we two were graying had changed our dispositions in the space of our small home and small rooms.

As years passed, we more generously imagined each other in readiness for further erasure.

Her eyes were green as acorn buds. The green of the veins in her mottled hands could be described with the very same pigment stain.

A wish

If, from memory, I was to draw my wife's wineglass wrong, the perfect base would seem to be sliding off or floating at a tilt from the surface of the bedside table.

If I were to draw the glass almost right, an unnatural disturbance in the falling-leaves pattern of our wallpaper would result.

If I were to commit to the interactions of the glass with the resistant and receptive forms of lamp and table and bottle— that is, if I were to draw rightly and wrongly—after all these years, I would be too insubstantial to be my own obstruction, and I could at last stop drawing what appears before me and could draw, as I truly wish, what reappears.

Oak

Unstable, unemployable, hungry and desperate for the most basic needs, unable to afford canvas, Chaim Soutine met with patrons kindly sent to him by his sometimes-friend Amedeo Modigliani. By prearrangement, Soutine brought a framed painting of an oak tree, which, so they wished, would be the first of their many purchases from him.

He did not tell them that "Oak" was an overpainting.

In order to save money on canvases, he often bought very cheaply the amateurs' lovingly rendered framed paintings always for sale at the junk markets, and he painted over.

In times of intensifying suffering, he painted over his own most successful attempts at "Hare on a Green Shutter," at "Return from School," at "Man Praying," at "The Polish Girl."

In a pinch or at a fit of pique, he painted over canvases friends had given him.

His loyal friend Modigliani painted many portraits of Soutine, and in these portraits he gifted Soutine with eyes instead of the blank sockets that were Modigliani's usual preference. The only one of these Modigliani portraits that Soutine had in his possession, he painted over. Over this portrait, which embodied Modigliani's fully realized mastery, Soutine painted an ancient mossy oak: the bleak open hand of the trunk at its center, the whirling branches expressively deformed by the faintest accidental suggestion of a man in his hiddenness—of Soutine—in a serene portrait pose. Soutine had impatiently, insufficiently, blotted himself out of context.

When the patrons began to pay him, he refused the large amount they offered, a charitable amount so great it insulted him.

He held the framed painting, taller than he, close to his body. He spoke from behind it.

"If you had given me one franc for my picture, I would have taken it," he told the wealthy woman and her husband, who found the painting unforgettably ugly, but who wished, after all, to please Modigliani.

(Sign above restroom urinal, Public Library,
Desordenada, North Carolina)

**The appearance of
The Deep Blue Sealant
rising up
through the drain holes
indicates the need
for** [illegible]

In the garden

Jesus is walking my neighborhood like he always does and he looks me in the eye, moves within arm's reach, says he needs me to drive him to his mother's.

And I say I don't have a car right now, and he says a sandwich would help him make the hard walk to her place—she's not well, she could use a sandwich too, and water you know.

And I say, "I don't know her or you, I'm not a sandwich man myself, you know—so: no."

He says he's got nothing against finger food.

He says, "D'you got pictures of your kids in your phone? How many've you got?"

No phone—car—kids? Let me guess. Three—and your oldest in his forties—like me. No pictures in your wallet?

None?

See, I'm sunsick, pain in my side, headache, bad feet, hands hurt. This trip home'll be long if I can't get a lift, and with no water sandwich friendship, I'll be in bad shape when I see my poor mother.

She's your age—seventy're thereabouts.

Got money to help her me us?

No?

So—you ever see your future self, eye to eye in this garden?

A long walk from there to here from then to now.

I lived for a while like you live—in a tale. I moved from place to place but where could I live—me and my mother—after we moved and moved and got moved?

D'you know that there're people'll put you in their story song sculpture poem, your place in their gnome garden, and pay you nothing for your face?

Who knows all this? Who?

You had a mother? She had a car? 'D she ever make you sandwiches, pour you the cool water the real love the juice to live—you know—when you were thirsty? 'D she clothe you school you clip your hair drive you safe everywhere you wanted?

Got one slice of bread one five-dollar bill? One spigot? God knows you got one—and good for you.

Before I go could I drink from your garden hose?

Passerby

We Passersby, Man in Fedora and Second Beat Cop and First Editions and Late Novels and The Eight and Barbara Stripe and Couple with Newspaper and Flapper Mannequin and Alabaster Mannequin and First Beat Cop and Parked Cabbie and Trench Coat Man, watched Mr. Kelly dance in the fake evening rain full of milk that gave the splashes lunar luster. The combination of midday sun and seasonal breeze caused the black tarpaulins covering the two-block movie set to luff, to momentarily leak sunlight, to mesmerize the light from streetlamps and storefronts, from mannequin skin, from oiled overcoats and high-gloss high dress shoes.

Mr. Kelly did not dance against the rainstorm but inside it. For ten days of rehearsal and seven days of filming and six hours a day of fake rain, he danced in and farther in. The director, the costume and set designers, the presoaked and resoaked Passersby in the choreographed number, all followed his maniacally focused control. At his insistence, all living and inanimate figures appearing with him would cue in strictly according to the little vamp upon which he had built every jazz-ballet-tap element. Do *dee* do de do dee—do *dee* do de do *dee*. He knew exactly how he would alchemize the camera's tracking of his five-minute progression inside the small storms of his character Don's joyous movement away from Kathy's door, and into his twelve duets with the Passersby, and down the *sss*sidewalk and across the flooded street and, at last, out of view.

The Passersby like me were expected to be *on* his precise beat of the little vamp during our seconds-long encounters with him. Mr. Kelly reminded us that the singing, dancing character named Don Lockwood was dancing with everybody and everything in his world, and he asked, "Do you get it?" The Passersby had to acknowledge we got it or suffer his withering shrug and glare and maybe even a terrible reminder that we were replaceable, that we were the fringe of the third-tier support for the people in the third- and fourth-tier supporting roles.

Don and Kathy's kiss lasts for five swells and a crescendo of violin music. She lifts his collar as she asks him to "take care of that throat. You're a big singing star now—remember?"

"Really?" he asks. The movie's whole premise is that Don and everyone like him are obsolete in the new movie industry, which, under the Oz-like power of Technicolor, is impatient to be rid of the hangers-on from the silent pictures era and the pretelevision moment. Don understands that no enterprise is more illusory than the American illusion business, but he has fallen in love with Kathy Selden and knows for sure that it's possible to be happy again. "Really?" he asks Kathy, and says, "From where I stand the sun is shining all over the place."

Do I, a Passerby, know all of Don's and Kathy's lines?

Really?

There isn't a line in the scene or a phrase of the whole song we Passersby don't know. This is a jukebox musical, after all, hammered together for the sake of refeaturing popular old songs that could be made new again on the old lots that are— that were—our haunts.

Almost fifteen seconds after their kiss, Kathy, dressed in a golden-yellow raincoat, slowly, reluctantly, retreats into the golden light of her apartment hallway and closes the gold-tinted glass door. Don lingers on the third step of the stoop, and has started to walk down and away when Trench Coat Man jogs past.

Trench Coat Man's shoulders slightly rotate toward Don who has begun to sing, "Do *dee* do de do dee—do *dee* do de do *dee*." There are twelve quarter notes in this bit, and it has taken Trench Coat Man repeated rehearsal efforts to stay on tempo. He's got it: do *dee* do dee do dee—clutch your collar—do dee do dee do—look over your shoulder, rush off to wherever you're rushing, Mister. This time, he's got it, and the sigh that almost invisibly lifts his shoulders seems like an effect Mr. Kelly wanted from him all along. We Passersby and all the company of actresses and actors hold Mr. Kelly in awe, understand that he is Don Lockwood, he really is Don, that it is 1951 at home and 1929 on the lot; the world of '51, certain that another war cannot reach this shore, is enthralled by the new magic of television and is ready to sit at table and at set and grow fat; the world of '29 goes nowhere while hurrying, while hurrying up and waiting, while wondering how to get out of the devastating storms of the Depression and the Pandemic and the torrential floods of Wounded and Dead.

Don rotates three hundred and sixty degrees and steps onto the fourth step, finger-waving to Trench Coat Man, their duet over in a measure excruciatingly endless to all the Passersby watching from the apron of the set, aware that Trench Coat Man must soon double up as one of Couple with Newspaper.

Don waves away Parked Cabbie. Waves him away and away and a-*way* until he finally drives off, rain guttering from the cloth roof of the De Soto. Go on, would you? Why would I need you? Good-bye, Parked Cabbie. Hey now—we nailed our duet in one take, didn't we?

First Beat Cop taps his truncheon against the black glove of his open, dripping palm. No more than a fireplug to Don, First Beat Cop moves on. First Beat Cop's left heel pushes forward, and then his right toe, feet closing: a waltz he makes look unrehearsed; he can do this better than most since he was Chaplin's assistant in 1914, assigned to drill everyone in scene with Chaplin during shooting of *The Tramp*. He was credited as Movement Specialist.

In Don's duet with the storefront Alabaster Mannequin bust in the golden blouse, she raises her elegant, bare arms to link her plaster hands with Don. She wants to be danced out of the smothering gold silk bunting, out from under the golden cloth tied in a butterfly knot, out from display. She isn't going anywhere, of course.

In the group of other nervous Passersby waiting for our moment in the lights, First Beat Cop mutters, "She's too much woman for Don."

Don lifts his hand up to let the rain hit there. He glances at his umbrella. What's the point? He folds it up, swings it onto his right shoulder. Trench Coat Man is in the shot again, still running down the sidewalk behind Don. For the sake of continuity, he has to run in place, more or less.

Don has already begun his duet with Flapper Mannequin in the next window down, another glowing-golden world behind glass uncannily reflective. He mirror-dances with himself there. Why would he dance in the rain anywhere, anyhow, with anyone else? Flapper's still ghost resigns more than approves. Her gold shoes glimmer. She freezes the shimmy-shake that lifts her hip and shivers her whole body, and Don shimmies to mock her and pay tribute.

Don leaps up onto the base of a streetlamp, holds on with his right hand, swings once, twice, leans out, crooks his left leg behind his right, leaps off, embraces the post as if ready to leap back on. He rests his smiling face against the column. The Passersby off set, who have now seen this bit more than other bits, are fairly indifferent to the startling, silly, ecstatic beauty. Our duets with Don: that's what holds our attention.

Couple with Newspaper, holding one flimsy sheet of *Variety* high over their heads, quick-steps toward Don. "Hold the paper—*hold* the damn paper—got it?" Mr. Kelly says. "Wind is under it. Feel that? You got to be wetter—Walt, wet them— that piece of paper's for absolutely nothing, and the couple just don't get it—got it?" Their arms have to stream with rain the headlines can't protect them from. The woman's hair- sprayed helmet hairdo should glisten. Walk walk walk walk walk walk, turn upper body, "Together now: turn—no—the upper body, I said—you listening?—Don is melting them. Try that. Melt that turn. Melt, for Christ's sake."

After another six takes, Couple with Newspaper dances the simple quick-step dance with Don. As far as Don's concerned, they're only two douses of rain he has passed. They walk, *rise-* walk walk-splash walk-splash walk-splash out of frame. He finger-waves to them, lifts off his hat, spreads his arms to wel- come more rain on his whole wool suit and dark tie and blue shirt. "Come on with the *rain*—I've a smile on my face."

Now, the stylized emptying of rain from inside his hat. Now, the Chaplinesque twirl of his closed umbrella.

At the Smoke MAHOUT display window under the PHARMACY awning is the poster of a young woman in a red-and-white barber-striped bathing suit top and blue high-waisted shorty shorts. The cig in her right hand is attached to a long holder. Egyptian obelisks flank her. Under them, small pharaoh silhouettes shamelessly fixate on her bare legs. Barbara Stripe—her credit designation—has the seductive power of a way-over-wonderful pinup on the nose of an Allied bomber, but she can't claim Don's attention.

He's in a rotating bowlegged step-and-sway with the imaginary partner that is the umbrella. He strums the umbrella to set the tune and tempo of his full tap routine. Swirling the umbrella in the air, he sailor-steps on the sidewalks in loud splashes, twirls the tip of it on the ground, twirls it over his head and stands under the gushing gutter spout before rushing into the street.

Enough with the umbrella: that's what some of the Passersby think, who know well that we're not paid to think.

In solitary rituals of trying-on, the group of eight smiling mannequin women in the LaValle Millinery Shop wear hats so out of fashion they might as well be crochet tea cozies or Caddy hubcaps. The light gold curtain behind them hangs flat as a cheap theater scrim. Figuratively and literally, The Eight are busts. Their expressive hands and long fingers touch the feelings they size up, their lifted pale-gray arms in a formal dance that does not include Don.

In front of the NCOTT Bookstore—as much as we can see of it—Don is still dancing "down the lane" with the same damn "happy refrain." The staid left-facing front window advertises LATE NOVELS; the right, FIRST EDITIONS. J.B. Lippincott's roaring volumes are, for Don, only backdrop: Ernest, Langdon, Edith, T.S., F. Scott. How can Don be happier than he was a block ago? Despite themselves, the scribblers've made him so! Don shuffles, do dee do dee do glides, spins, stomps quick-stomps stomps stomps stomps glides into a crisscross Charleston freight-training past every stepper who has ever been not quite in step.

MOUNT HOLLYWOOD and ART SCHOOL signage appear as flimsy afterthought. They were the sites of peak faith experiences we barely remember now, having been in the countless pilgrimages of pretending that have ended where they started. Duet with Second Beat Cop begins with Don blocked by the tall man in the black oilcloth overcoat, shining badge worn on the outside.

The camera has glided up above them both. On beat, Second Beat Cop crosses his arms, follows Don in from the street, looks down at Don who slightly, slightly leans forward in a kiss-me-if-you-will gesture, and pivots around the tall copper whose rain-struck hat material spangles with spreading and disappearing stains.

Second Beat Cop, whose real name is Oscar, knows how many beats to hold in place. He holds. He holds. In other movies, Oscar has been the piano player or has been the uncredited piano hands standing in for nonmusician actors. For this duet Mr. Kelly has coached Oscar to look-and, to look-and, and to look long, with pleasure-taking but not scene-stealing intensity, with dawning appalled astonishment at Don walking in strides of travel-rocking and basic running, out of the law's reach. Twice, Don waves good-bye. Good-bye, Oscar. Good-bye, Second Beat Cop.

Off set, Parked Cabbie and Couple with Newspaper hug Second Beat Cop, who has nailed his duet with Don, just nailed it airtight. They are silent embraces. From this, the coffin of the last industry job he'll ever have, Second Beat Cop nods at Man in Fedora—that's me—like he wants to supportively say, "Do me one better."

To do anyone one better is not the job, I'm proud to say.

I stride in polite businesslike strides, my brown long coat leaden, my focus on the ground. I'm marching toward Don at the moment; he's mugged the cop and caromed off him and danced down the sidewalk for our duet.

Under my fedora, pulled down almost onto the bridge of my nose, I'm humming the little vamp, and I think I hear Mr. Kelly's vamp marking time as Don walks toe *heel* heel heel heel *toe*—a man no television set could ever contain, and no color capture, and no dime unlock from the jukebox—on a collision course straight at me. The rain hasn't become gentler. The rain is modulating differently than in the eleven duets before this one. The downpour is tapping at the whole world in exactly the rubato sound we heard when Don and Kathy kissed.

In less than a quarter note, Don has pressed his umbrella into the center of my chest and, holding the hinge of it to swing around me, he is gone, more gone, gone out of sight and off set.

He knows, and all the Passersby know, this is the part I always screw up. I hear Mr. Kelly, standing off set but very close, sternly say, "Now," and I imagine Don say, "Open."

* * *

At the perfect moment, I opened the black canopy of the umbrella. I looked down into the underside—with happiness I'll never know how to explain—and I thought, *This* is how I matter—before lifting the flimsy thing over me.

I strode toward Couple with Newspaper standing together ten feet off the set, who danced crazily with me and my umbrella partner for one full rotation. Second Beat Cop and Parked Cabbie slapped my soaked shoulders. First Beat Cop kindly truncheoned me on my heart.

What are we given that honors when and how we gave, we Passersby?

Watch my nine seconds again, would you?

(DDS 800.001, book spine, Public Library,
Desordenada, North Carolina)

**One
Touch
Response**

In the Gila

In the Gila Wilderness at sunrise on the West Fork, I walked in small strides through knee- and waist-high warm ash that steamed me in my boots and waders. The slightest fall wind sent light ash onto my pack, my glasses, face, hair, my back and chest. In my camp, I couldn't completely remove the ash-coat even on the lower half of me that was hard-washed by river crossings.

Returning to the ranger's station three days later, I asked, "What was *that*?" and pointed to the hiking trail on the glossy large-scale map.

He said, "Hello!" and paused unnaturally as one would at an animated gray ghost.

His finger touched my finger on the map. He lifted his uniform hat without removing it, and said again, "Hello!"

He said, "You're not going to believe me." He wanted me to read his clean wrist and hand and finger, I guessed. Or he wanted me to hear the authority in his voice. Or he wanted me to read his face.

"That fire was three years ago," he said. "The map won't show that."

*   *   *

I returned to the same location in winter. The sleigh bell on the ranger station door rang when I stepped in.

I said hello to the same ranger. He was wearing a sleigh bell as a kind of bolo tie.

He lifted his uniform hat, said, "Hello there!"

"I'm back," I said. I'm fairly sure I was talking more to me than to him. "I'm going back in."

"Map?" he asked. Our fingers touched the eight-mile stretch on the giant map, the glass newly cleaned. We could see each other in the sunrise gloss where time marked us as vague glowing shapes superimposed over place names and trails and ruins and winding rivers. You'd think I would've noticed his nametag.

He sternly warned me against cross-country skiing that part of the Gila after the recent massive snowstorm. Apparently forgetting he was a younger man speaking to an elder, he said, "Anyway—remember: no shame in turning back."

When I thanked him, giving no indication I would take his advice, the odd fellow said, "Same as ever."

Through the window of the station, he watched me make a test run in the snow of the empty parking lot to sense the camber of my skis and to take the measure of the distance I could go.

That morning and afternoon, I skied into the same section of the Gila. No one had tracked in, so I broke fresh snow, congratulating myself on moving through the brightness fairly lightly and capably for a man unaccustomed to it.

The river whistled against frozen banks, the way that sharp blades sing from tempered sheaths. Glistening pines, diminutive, poked through more perfect in their forms than any I had ever seen. When I brushed against one, a cleansing fragrance shivered from the whole multitude surrounding me. Why had I not given more attention to them—so many, so young—in my previous journey? I supposed that in the earlier hike, the ashes and the swarming, biting flies hatching in the radiating ash-heat had distracted me from more sensitive observing.

I returned at sunset to the station. The jingling door closed behind me; the jingling ranger called out, "Hello!" apparently pleased that I had not inconvenienced him by dying.

Comically, I couldn't summon an answering hello. The silence that penetrated me out there had dissolved my insistent need to speak.

"Well?" he asked.

"Well?" I asked back.

I wanted to know about the expansive fields of splendid pines, a dreamlike aspect I couldn't put out of mind. "What was *that*?" I asked, my finger pushing against the map.

A ranger, whose job requires kind responsiveness, can easily be mistaken for a friend.

"*That*," he said, not returning my smile, "that was something you've never seen—and you never will. You're too small in the big picture of things at the unimaginable scale—no insult intended—and you don't see what you should."

He looked at the wall clock in an end-of-shift glance. The glass face was polished. The black steel cage locked over it was polished. I wondered whether I had ever once in my life been so conscientious as he.

He said, "They're the crowns of pines under snow. Tons and tons of snow."

I said, "Snow."

He said, "Yeah," thrusting a hand toward me and taking mine up to make me shake. With his other hand on my back, he moved me out toward my car.

The ranger shut off the lights inside and out. When he locked the door, a shushing sound came from the station, an echoing, sealing sound from the surrounding forest.

The headlights of his car swept the lot and me and the darkness around me.

*　*　*

In the spring, ten years later, I brought my former self to visit the Gila.

I'm not sure I know what I mean by that.

I brought the older man still marked by the younger.

No.

No to that romantic bullshit.

I brought new understanding of obliterated marriage, family, friendship, the expired fellowship of acquaintances: the self-estrangements that result from divorce, pandemic, death, forced retirement, detachment.

No.

No to "understanding" any of it.

The trails lost, buried, burned, I came in order to bring my wilderness to this wilderness.

No.

No to that assessment's shapeliness, the kind of thing one writes who is the sole audience for anything he writes.

I was, in fact, an ignorant young and lost wanderer who had become an ignorant lost and old wanderer.

The ranger said, "You again," and I knew I could not explain to him the several selves I brought.

He must have thought he understood. "Do you recognize me?" he asked, pushing at but not removing his hat.

I said, "Of course."

He said, "No—no—I mean: me."

Ridiculous, I thought, of course I do.

Then, conceding he might be asking something else, I lied, said, "Yes."

He stood too close, said, "First time you came in I remembered: you gave me a 'D' in Freshman Composition. Thirty-one years ago."

When was that? I thought. When was that?

I was probably the reason he landed in this remote station. Our chance meeting now had probably brought old sorrows back to him. He probably pictured himself haunted by me in the future when I would return like a curse season after season.

No, I thought. No to all those narcissistic judgments.

His laughter sounded like snow shrugging from a roof in rapid stages of letting go.

He brought me a coffee and sat next to me with his.

He neither broke his silence, nor implied that I must break mine. He returned my smile with the gracious, reassuring smile mandatory for a forest ranger, for a person seeing so few humans that the encounters matter immeasurably.

How on earth can some things—no, all things—be forgiven all at once and for always?

We both stared into the face of the giant map, which comprehensively marked particular physical features of the Gila but inaccurately represented the vastness.

The ranger asked, "Same route?"

Poise

Fifth position. Adjust. Knees unlocked. Only barely. Weight forward. Butt and head aligned. Adjust. Shoulders down. Left shoulder joint drawn back but not like that. Gaze fixed. Adjust. Neck lifted. Lifted better. Upper chest expanded. Left ribcage projected slightly. Arms reaching out, roundly.

You've never held this form of roundness? Adjust. Elbows out, aligned with shoulders. Center of back contracting. Left hand and wrist adjusted to partner's hand. Frame pressed forward, upward.

Can you grow that movement? Grow it. Heel of right palm firm against partner's side. Right fingers under partner's shoulder blade. Adjust her.

Now you.

Now the two.

Frame lightly pulled back with heel and palm of right hand. Adjust.

Imagine a window over her right shoulder. No seeing yourself there. No softening your craggy face's expression. Have you seen this view before?

And farther from this window, another appears.

Another farther on.

Beyond the lines of dance, a larger, clearer window opens. A younger you climbs through with one basic, one half of one full rotation, one inside spin, one outside, one flying change-turn.

Adjust.

Adjust beyond performing adjustments.

Find perfect fifth again.

Stop, old man.

Just stop.

Stop.

Stop adjusting.

Beyond judges, judgments, limits: your old body hovers above itself rhythmically aware and ready as a bell rung by a breeze, limbs letting go one shore of sound for this one, losing the full gown of earth for sleeves of sun, for head attuned to hers, hips tilted back in time.

All bearing spaces between are unburdened, your hearts free from their thrones, your unreposed bodies poised in the unrobing, the diving down, the upreaching coming after long dormancy.

Let us draw near

"No day shall erase you from the memory of time,"
Virgil, *The Aeneid*, National September 11 Memorial Museum

Ten days after 9/11, my father's heart exploded, his life collapsing in a matter of moments. We could not find each other in our own familiar streets. We could not ask now how to meet him in the ash. Old-school Catholics, we prayed, "Adiemus. Adiemus."

There were two of me, one loving, one late in loving. I set aside the national mourning, which I could not withstand. When you said he can rest now, asked how you could help, that brought no calm, and no peace came when you recalled your own lost ones.

No new perspective came when the news returned again, again to the three thousand gone, to acts of heroism, to horrors visited upon survivors, to tender personal interviews news cycle after news cycle that I took in while ignoring, ignoring the entire wrecked nation.

Today my sister, youngest of the five children, has died before her turn. She has ended her participation in our grim middle-age sibling tag game of electronic messaging, burning each other with teasing grief, our way to touch but not be done with familial anniversaries of mistaking one obliterated story for another.

How many further words are farther out of reach. How few near are terribly nearer. The expression of tribute the nation leaves for the nation is Virgil's martial words, as out of context as severed heads in snow. No monuments stand long, and in that I find consoling bitter satisfaction.

Ten days after your deaths (and only incidentally your lives) were lovingly commemorated, I did, I did turn off the tube, unplugged you three-thousand dead from my living memory.

The two of me, one loving and one late in loving, called to mind their names, words towering over all other inscriptions. Hers was Wendy, meant to echo his. Wendell.

The parable of the robe

During the apportioning ritual he had asked—he had been the only one to ask—for the royal blue robe with the unusual high collar and the dense material at the chest and waist and weighted hem. The robe included cleverly installed inseam snap buttons. Sturdy belt loops remained in place for a missing wide leather cinch.

Snug on him as a skin, it fit, it really fit: an actual skin with blemishes, with cloth smelly from the house's unguents and rank cushions, and from the smoke and the animal renderings of past houses, and from the oils and from the coals and from the larded molds and sewer-gases and moth balls and dander smears and vinegars of structures older yet.

Snug on him. An old man in his old man's blue-rat outfit: he felt the descendant's pride in claiming this dressy gown his father wore that had been grandmother's and inherited from her father who had worn the robe passed down for generations, sometimes to a woman, sometimes to a man.

He shucked his pants and socks and shirt and entered again: enrobed as if enthroned, the air around him heating and expanding.

This, he thought, is how the dead warm the living.

In his tight-fitting housedress, he regally strode and danced awhile, processed ungrandly up and grandly down the staircase, bowed to and boogied with the stout sylvan-green fridge. He felt of his time and not, of his gender and the other, of his own self-constructions and of his secret nature.

As his siblings had scattered out and away with their new possessions, saying good-bye good-bye to the eight hundred square feet of sentiment, he had waved at them, welcoming their laughter at the absurd ruff collar swamping him, the once-handsome robe sleeves waggling, his tiny, mighty paws retreating: son inside his father's mother's father, man in a man's woman's man's rags, rat in a rat's rag's rat's rags, years upon years of recompense for abundances and impoverishments.

The way that a rat chuckles, he chuckled; he grinned, pretended he was wearing smooth and hairy ears, hairy and smooth shoulders, his waist tightly belted and full breasts lifted, pretended it suited him fine to be so coarse, so fair.

The rough boards and uneven tiles and dust-gummed carpets bit and snipped at and bristled under his bare feet. At the crumby corners of the rooms, he bowed to get the drift again of the unsettled complaints, the settled ones, the matters of dispute utterly ill-suited to one moment inherently tailored to the next.

Rat to rat, we can at last be at peace, he thought.

He stripped off his boxers, shirked himself further into this new old way of inhabiting a story about being neither and becoming both, apart from and of one part of dim and vivid recognition.

He sat. Between his knees, he made a robe-cloth basin into which the tears that would hit hit hit and sink in could be passed down.

(Public Library, Desordenada, North Carolina.
Underlined, in
Parts of Speech: The Genet Practical Guide)

<u>*when* modifies the verb *flee*</u>

Cake all day

When he visited her at Jeta's Grove Care Center, he stayed for an hour, at most two. He brought her outside in her grand throne, a cross between a La-Z-Boy and a wheelchair. Her light robe was neatly arranged behind her shoulders. Underneath her were neatly tucked sheets and rubber sheets and a bottom layer of foam padding.

He closed the sliding doors of the sunporch behind them, and she arranged herself, lifting her back and turning slightly to take pressure off her left leg, shifting the position of her left arm on its special pillow. Left arm and left leg, which were of no use since her stroke one year ago, were a source of constant and passing sadness to Dorothy Eva. She understood that her leg and arm were eighty-year-old rememberers.

She had a view.

In her company on the sunporch, he had a view, too.

They sat together in peculiar abandonment of politeness and in unique attunement particular to their relationship. Their respectful disregard-deep-regard for each other was made possible by the porch, a place of refuge that faced the Blue Ridge mountains bowing their mist-cloaked heads and shoulders in successions of vigor and humility.

The weekly visit was entirely devoted to cake. All day the two offered different kinds of imaginary cake, inquired about the cake of everyone they encountered, engaged each other in discussions of the ultimate cake, inquired about the teaching of cake, about the lineage of cake makers, about the mysterious companionship of those who seek to partake with others in cake. Cake was convincing evidence that God existed: The Baker.

Much of their time together was spent in simply being attentive to each other's self-talk. About cake, of course. Who else but Dorothy Eva permitted him to audibly share his self-conversation? He thought aloud: "Start me off with a small piece. We'll. I'll. Another is better than stopping at one. She'll tell you that. It's a fact, it's a. Fact. I'll tell you if it's got icing piled up to heaven, we'll I'll she'll eat off that part or bite by bite steal the cake. Down to the crumbs. Steal the cake from the icing so the walls of icing stand up clean, not even cake crumbs in it! She'll say spoon. I say fork. Spoon? Really? The walls of icing stand up like something great, some tiny great ruins on some uncrumbed, totally unbelievably uncrumbed plate. The walls. The icing walls stand up so you hate to eat them. Like the cake never was there waiting to be forked spooned. Ate. You have to, have to eat the cake walls last. She'll. I'll."

They did not ask each other to clarify what they overheard. They did not interleave; that is, one did not stream thought aloud into the other's thought. They took turns witnessing, alert in the listening.

This particular April First was only different than the other days because on this day his heart would not start, would crank, crank-cough, almost rev, crank, stop, go silent, go down beyond recharging in the Center's parking lot right after his visit with Dorothy Eva during which every cell of him had been recharged with life and had seemed to hold the charge but in one gasp-laugh-cough had gone silent.

On the porch, inside their co-echoing, he listened to her thought: "Give them will you some of this delicious, will you give them their slices—they change me, bring me extra toast pills medicine for sleep or pain or nothing—they got a crane to put you in—if you don't have one get one a them for your bath—the operator lifts you out you go out you go out—into the air you swing, you rock back—up—back—you land in warm towels, fresh—the clothes are fresh so fresh—they like cake like you like cake—they like cake—will you will you— we—he—we'll have the whole thing we like—he—comes here, must be has to can't be—he—you know you know what, you know what?—you know him?—he—someone like him comes, we have the kinds we like and not the kinds we don't when he comes here—we—"

Often, a nurse would check on them, a gardener would wave, a porch encroacher (a crow or squirrel) would attempt to encroach.

He said to the crows, "We're down to the icing." The crows cocked their blue-black heads. Their talons, like trigger fingers, curved into the grass under which were thick buttercream worms. Each crow bowed and rocked in private but unquiet prayer.

She asked the laundry service delivery person if she was delivering more cake in cake boxes on cake carts from cake crates unloaded from the cake ships. "Ports," she said, thinking of sunlight sliding through sliding doors her chair could slide through, thinking of him, her visitor, standing there, sitting near.

On this particular day, she asked, "Do you have a favorite?" and the laundry deliverer, her ears and eyebrows and nose lobes shining with decorative metal, who had been there many times, cheerily said, "German chocolate with milk chocolate pecan frosting!"

Dorothy Eva asked, "Got a crane?" The craneless young woman smiled blankly.

Dorothy Eva said, "Crane's a good thing."

He said to the crows, "You don't like icing, I see."

Neither of them needed to tell the crows to go on now, off the porch. The cawing fray jumped swooped swept back into the cirrus The Baker had spread across the skies for them.

She said, "Wrong porch," to Nurse, who had opened the screen doors and peeked her whitecapped head out to bring water in a kind of sippy glass and pills in a tiny pleated cup.

He said, "Wrong porch" in solidarity with Dorothy Eva.

"Swallow, Miss," Nurse, faster than the fastest avoiders, said.

Though no swallows came to the porch, there was no reason for Dorothy Eva or him to think they never could. He said, "Could be," and Dorothy Eva said, "Sure could," and she offered cake to the nurse, who explained that she was watching her weight, and said, "We need to change you, Miss," and could not dodge the broom of their thoughts (Done swallowing. Done. Didn't see it all go down?) coming at her, and said, "Later," and, reading their reaction, said, "Not a lot later."

A floater, a frequent visitor in veiled form, arrived in Dorothy Eva's peripheral vision, and leaped and cavorted there with fitful light pulses. Her face heard her stomata calling inside her orbital cavities: the lustrous pourings-in of noise hardening into sound, of sound into song, of song cracking and cooling glassily.

She said, "Put a knife in—see if—" He said, "—comes out gluey—" She said, "—melts—" and thought aloud, "Hard to hear-see with you stabbing my cake."

He said, "Floater, eh?" He thought aloud, "Your face!" and looked not a moment longer than she would wish, and thought, Everything is there, and said quietly to her, his sister, his dearest friend in all his long life: "You have an everything face, Dear."

She showed him herself in her face, said, "I guarded pyramids for centuries with this."

He looked, making sure she could hear his awe as he thought, You are dear, Dorothy Eva.

A tree in the garden rustled in an upspeaking breeze touching leaf stems and leaf buds, the touching ending with rising-pitch intonations: the breeze-strokes asking questions.

The old gardener's unanswered cell phone warbled to them, stopped, and warbled more playfully.

The gardener's mother lived at Jeta's Grove. In order to be near her, he volunteered in all seasons. He told Dorothy Eva and him once—because, of course, they asked him for cake wisdom—that a slab of cake too big and a little too warm and another slice possible is a boy's greatest object-experience of love.

Across the old slopes, cloud-shreds glided down and seemed to bring hairbrush and wind-engine and grocery cart and truck traffic sounds that unraveled and raveled inside the porch.

His construction crew of work-worn and dirty men bounded from the memory of Dorothy Eva and him at the same moment. The two made conversation that loosely recapitulated the week-ago conversation the men and he and Dorothy Eva had about their mothers and the cakes their mothers made of the tiered and untiered varieties.

And they had talked about the gold you panned for in the bottom of the cake pan. One man, the oldest of the crew, said, "That dough rind you got after everybody got their pieces out. I'd get a stiffy smelling that. Oh, Lord," and the crew all said, "Oh, Lord!", every one of the men more or less needing their drawers changed.

He and his building crew had made simple, inexpensive two-stories that community members liked for their trademark poetical roof parapets. In such fairytale abodes, the pomeowners could laugh at the delusions of protection that come with walls and roofs and the footings upon which assumptions of ownership and certainty are constructed. After his retirement, his men remained loyal friends, and they stayed near in his thoughts and, so, hers.

Nurse was not at all surprised that Dorothy Eva responded the next day to the news of his death by saying, "Plenty of cake everywhere all the time, you know us, you know we have the kind we like. Want some?"

Nurse wheeled her onto the porch where she had a view, where he had had a view, too, and where they had shared cake all day.

This account of Dorothy Eva and her brother-in-law is not about one of two unsilenced people silencing, is it?

This thing has been poured into and removed from a form.

This thing of a few words, and far too few.

This is the cake The Baker made who wanted above all else to create one taste, another taste, a sweetness.

Sharpied on the inside lid of a hatbox

This crèche will make nothing happen when you take the fourteen parts from the hatbox and unwrap the news of '42 covering 1) the manger made of tongue depressors given to Grandmother as a small child for sticking her tongue so far out and saying ahh and not dying except almost many times later from her miscarriages. Unwrap the tissue paper around 2) Joseph & donkey & 3) lamb & 4–6) three camels & 7–9) three empty-handed Wisemen & 10) Mary & infant-cemented-in-crib. Item 11) is the model race car brought by her wayward grandson out of prison in '97. Hesitantly welcomed home, Frank introduced 12) the fourth Wiseman who wears a long, striped robe and is swaddled in 13) a hand-inked handkerchief drawing of King Herod. Seek until you find 14) the blue starbulb that fits the manger's roof hole. See, Assembler, you have proven nothing at all by bringing light here for a little while.

Sharpied on a damaged MAGA car windshield

I can explain this—I walk our neighborhood with a pickaxe as company, good for destruction or protection but heavy—this terror is an Act of God you could say, if you were an insurance agent or arch evangelist—I do not employ this weapon unless necessary—satisfying to use but unwieldy, my immigrant grandmother left it to me—I don't mean she was unwieldy or heavy or good for destruction or protection. She was though— before breakfast with my grandfather, before giving birth, before bar hours or night class, before church or auto service or after a wedding or divorce in the family or parish wake or an election day or fourth of July—she never said to me, "I have only this one pickaxe" because she had many—the note she left me said, "This here will come in handy at the right moment in history when racist religious fascists place themselves everywhere: every school, every church, every parking space"—an axe a pick a long thick handle rough grip, she taught me force precision speed grit—I don't mean she was speedy precise a spiritual force a handshake or oak handle or pick or axe—she was though—"You will regret it if you leave any inch undamaged," she said—who knows how much injury can be done in a short while with the exact right domestic tool—Grandmother knew—I know—now you do too.

Around my bed America was falling

Thank you for the four years I have been owned by The White Noise Machine, which has helped me sleep in oblivion. I couldn't have known the sleep a natural-born American man can find who each night listens with calming satisfaction to the sounds in the noise, to the pleas and the cries. I couldn't have known that overwhelmed by human misery, I could crash so far down into dream, a full-sail man blown at amazing acceleration—beautiful, so beautiful—past the youngest of the children taken from their families, given no information, shown no path home, thrown as pawns into pens, their stories, their living stories buried in mass graves almost pandemic-vast. I feel so blessed to have this winning White Noise Machine, a hoax-cast of compost orange, dialing me in, protecting me from exhausting consciousness, from sleep-destroying impulses of wide-awake conscience. During this nightly terror briefing I can be lowered, my field of stripes and stars shaken, straightened, folded thirteen times, can sleep just fine tucked into my locked display case, and not have to be a human tossing and turning, trying to know his own loving-learning mind. I like every single setting: Pray Them Dead Lock Them Up Wall Them Out Steal Their Vote Merika Mine Merika More Mine Merika All Mine. O, My Greatagain Merika! This is the most patriotic wreath you will ever sleep beneath!

Dr. Ivivi Adada's admonition

People talk who say they'll never tell—tell who say they'll never talk—say who say they'll never say—talk who will say they never will tell but will never say they never will tell.

People told who said they never would—talked said told who never could tell say talk the talk.

People told who never talked—people who—people who never said that people never would talk.

People say they said they say they talked, they talked they told they told they told they said so sadly.

People will, they say, not say talk tell ever tell talk.

So say people—people—all people.

Mr. Noom

In the university cubicle that was my nest I had as a friend a colorful, feathered parrot (Kmart, $12) (batteries included) suspended from my low ceiling on his own perch near my one, sealed office window. You could give him brief phrases that he would remember and speak back to you when you spoke to him.

Everything he said, he sang, and quite often it was the same thing: "Hello, you old fossil! HelLOW! HelLOW!"

He insisted upon monitoring my student conferences. "His eyes," student-parents would say when they brought their children. The children were drawn to the plastic, feather-coated creature, whom I had named Mr. Noom on a night of full moon that his refractive lenses had made into an other-moon.

The children helped me dust him and comb him and add to his vocabulary. In 1986 a child named Mota, Q-tipping Mr. Noom's grimy, hard plastic tongue, asked, "Is he Off—for sure?"

* * *

If the phone rang when he was On, he sang-rang in response. He sang-knocked at the sound of a door knocking; he sang-rained in the monsoon season. The children liked how his eyelids clicked closed, clacked open as he swung, dipped up, dipped down. He had too many talons, ten, but the children and I did not consider this a terrible disadvantage.

You could not erase from his speech anything that Mr. Noom had learned, since he had no Erase function. I could never understand how his so-called Vital Initiating Mechanism prevented Mr. Noom from reciting every time all the words and sounds he had ever learned through the time of his life as a manufactured alien.

He had not come with a preprogrammed tone. He could not change his open nature, though his Vocal Speed and Movement settings were variable.

We liked him low and slow, the children and I, the students and I, my own children and I, I and the teacher I strove to become.

Like all of us, he had a "running time." His was about eighteen minutes before his batteries would need to be recharged or replaced.

How many thousands of hours of student conferences did I have with Mr. Noom present? Is it possible that at least some of the students recognized that I was an imposter-teacher, not mentally well or, for that matter, not *fit* to teach?

There were thousands of students.

There have been so many names in so many gradebooks.

There was a mother and a child, a father and a child.

There always will be.

Mota and I and her mother—who was very young, though no younger than I or Mr. Noom—liked Mr. Noom. We liked him odd, kind, liked him aware, awake. He was curiously calming, disturbing.

We liked how his memory was set. His manner seemed set, too, but I recognize now that assumption was an illusion.

After you had self-confessed, he confessed your sins to you, absolving them more or less. After you had begun weeping, he wept with you. When you continued laughing, he echoed back exactly how you had laughed.

When it seemed my solitude would not leave, he stayed. When it seemed no solitude could hold, he stayed but seemed to leave.

In the quiet he fell quiet, in the way that a sentence can fall quiet behind a preposition. Because of the quiet in my home after our adult children left the nest. Because of the damning quiet of my wife in our empty house. Because of the absence of friends whom I ignored in order to write. Because of the death of my physical health under the pressures of writing and teaching. Because of books I wrote that lived in boxes and teaching I did that lived in files. Because of the ones that died there. Because of the ones that didn't die, that lived by making sounds noise nonsense that caused people, including a handful of unstable readers engaged by each book, to ask, "What is it?"

Because of all this, when Mr. Noom fell quiet, I could feel myself breaking, that all my strained skull-seams were cracking.

*   *   *

Mr. Noom would permit us to play pretend games with him, but he particularly liked pretend eating.

"Don't mind if I do," he would sing to an offer of coffee, bit of rubber eraser, peanut-butter-and-jelly, potato chip, onion ring. "Meaningless food," he sang about celery sticks, "and healthy!" To a bean burrito Mota and her mother once offered him, he sang, hungrily, "Om. Om."

A starving person could not feel starved in Mr. Noom's presence, would not leave him feeling uncharitable toward the starving.

You could say—but you would find you were singing—that we loved him.

If you conversed with him long, you understood he sang instead of said because *you* did. Because you did, he tucked his head down, shuddered, asked about choosing paths of thought, about the mysteries of controlling or relenting expression, about his grade in Basic Composition, whether he would pass, whether he would not, whether he might simply run out before completing the course.

When you muttered and rocked with Mr. Noom, he rocked and muttered with his sharp bill closed in secret-keeping communion.

*   *   *

"Mota's daughter!" I sang to Mr. Noom in the fall semester of 2006 when the photo of the toddler grandchild came with the note: Mota's little one—Yedra. Mota missing three years now. There is a picture. And there is hope.

The students I taught had the opportunity to learn in my classroom that language subjectively *creates* what it names: *hope*, for instance. They learned that language objectively acknowledges the constructed reality before us: *missing three years* and *picture*. Language, I preached, summons for us what has been and what is coming: *little one*. Any expression of language asks us to respond (cerebrally, generally) and to react (viscerally, specifically) to the word-pouring and word-spilling that has evolved and devolved as living and fossilized utterances impossibly fly from inside us and from far inside us, and from far outside us (yet *of* us) at billions of frames per second that punctuation hardly slows down by more than nanoseconds. The rhetorical expression called "the existence condition"— *There is* or *There has been* or *There was* or *There will be*—reflects the condition of us hearing the noise or music of our words simultaneously composing and revising that condition.

I was a shitty gifted teacher. I was, more or less, a teacher going mad in the incomprehensibly spacious prison of language to which I had committed my life, believing that my vows were holy and that the servant life of the writer was ludicrously sacred.

Looking back on any moment of my life as a teacher and a writer, I see that I offered despairing and ecstatic madness.

* * *

There is madness.

There has been madness.

*　*　*

There was.

There will be.

"Read this poetry. I *ask* you. Read this," I said to a senior student, a Vietnam veteran, living in his car during his six years of study, working at night for Burger King.

In 2002 he majored in criminal science, certain that a job in Homeland Security would be open; he was right, of course, that his country would always hold this particular kind of job open for him. After he was hired, he came to visit, said hello to Mr. Noom, gave me $500 to repay me for the money I had included inside the pages of Yusef Kumenyaaka's *Neon Vernacular*. No mention of the poems. No description of his ICE job, which I believed—Christ, my beliefs were childish!—he never would have fit into at all if he had read the poems.

In 2008 he brought his three-year-old to meet Mr. Noom. The child lightly petted his dusty tail feathers, said, "Know tricks?" and Mr. Noom answered, "No tricks."

"Saved by *not* reading poetry," I said to Mr. Noom, after the soldier and his daughter left.

Without a hint of cynicism, Mr. Noom said, "Read this." After a bomb-ticking mechanical moment, Mr. Noom said, "I ask you. I *ask* you. I ask you."

*　*　*

If sometimes you failed to hit Off but wished to be Off, wished aloud to be free from the years of pretending to be fully sane, the years in which you, always the lifelike watcher, watched the young launch alive into the world with their young, Mr. Noom did not question that this was the service for which you were equipped, though his eyes, always jittery, might roll when you hit his On switch.

His eyes. His eyes.

When the grown children of my long-ago students visited me. When they came without their parents. When they came alone, I mean came to me when I was alone. When that happened, I would hear about their lives, so magnificent, aberrant, fulfilling, terrifying. When they left, I remembered their words. I could hardly bear how happy I was, how despairing. With great particularity, I remembered.

I paced my office. I called my wife to say I would be late. At a certain point, nothing pleased her more than knowing I would not be there.

I sat and wrote down some of their words. Some of my own, too. (I have done this all my life for no one. I do. I will.)

I said some of their words aloud. Some of mine.

He sang, "Mr. Noom! Hello, you old fossil!" but not in a self-introducing tone, not with his own inflection, but with mine. "HelLOW! HelLOW?"

Mr. Noom, my eccentric, durable office friend during my fifty years of open sky and of prison, that wondrous-dim, infinite, brief span.

Mr. Noom.

Mr. Noom.

Recommendation

My father, ex-employee, knows I haven't much to say on his behalf. An isolated musical genius. A monk, recently, of the Laughing-Face Order, until psylocibin in large doses brought early and sustained enlightenment. I cannot recommend that you ask him to refrain from enlightening. Greater than any innovator of his era, he can't make straight or curved lines of song but can find in the scrawl the quintessence of our human quivering at this trembling eon-hour. What good has it done him that he hears in the simplest instructions the bus-ride cymbal-sound tiss-tiss-tiss and the voices beneath passengers' voices and the syncopation in any worker's task, but is no good for finishing anything (his marriage even) you could ask of him?

I cannot recommend that you ask anything of the riddling old musician—he will reset the racking speed of every lane, the volume of the strike alarm; he will retune each sink in the Women's and Men's to hear their rushing harmonies; he will throw the bowling shoes at the pins and the pins at the score screens, and will rest the blue bowling balls in the ice from the ice machine, only for the sake of displacing.

He displaces (his children even). Even his own most promising gifts he (the brilliant other he) displaces. If he is what you hire, I ask you: What the hell have you got?

I cannot recommend that you ask him to place himself alone in your bowling alley where so many mirrors can be ghost-streaked, so many trophies can be dressed in doll clothing, so many team portraits polished, lipsticked, every lip and finger-tip and shoe tip, every hat replaced with one half of an idiotic un-hat-like Winkblot.

I cannot, in good faith, recommend that you hire this man (how has he lived so long?) (and why?), this dizzying, darkening well I know so well.

Do not.

Do not make the same mistake I made by hiring from within.

Monument Technologies, Inc.
Grave site bid, job no. 2024

Will grow your swimming pool and surrounding areas into monument site.

Will dismantle and remove conventional pool filtering machinery. Will provide centered explosive (thirty seconds in duration) memorial fountain set on once-a-month time schedule. Entrained to the schedule, insect hatches result, bird populations follow, nesting and seeding migration patterns occur, weather patterns alter.

Will replace all pool lights with mild waterjets (4) that rock newly planted lily pads (24) guarding proposed frogs (12), giant carp (10), monster catfish (8), mature snapping turtles (6), poisonous and nonpoisonous water snakes (48, total) stocked in five stages over ten-day period.

Will enmoss (Bryophyta, "Antarctic moss") the deck chairs (4) and diving board.

Will enmoss (same) the pool ladder rails, deck and apron, pool fence, pool house.

Will enmoss (same) the Pool Rules poster affixed to pool fence.

Will introduce a dune (2 dump truck loads, 15 tons) of black drift-grain consuming not quite all of existing round table and giant sunbrella. Drift-grain (organic) generates apparitions during mild and strong wind conditions, partially disappears from your memorial property, reappears whole or in part in nearby and globally distant open areas, reappears on your property as multiple dune-mounds and dune-berms.

Will enscum the surface of pool margins with rhizoids of bright jade algae (Rhodophyta, "Wand" algae) resisting and inviting diver-mourners and mourner-divers, human and animal.

Will secure by triple anchor your Waiting Chamber at pool bottom. Will microfossilize ("Red bed" rust) chamber surface.

Will install underwater bell. Bell tolls on death day, birthday. 165dB (amplitude of ALSOU, Afterlife Sonic Utterances).

Will complete job within thirty days after your death.

Will maintain until system self-perpetuates: approximately 10–12 months. Warranty expires at that time.

(Public library, Desordenada, North Carolina,
Circulation Desk, laurel oak wood, "1918, Mark 9:49"
engraved on pull plate of center drawer,
drawer four inches deep, forty-eight inches long,
filled with sea salt.)

To be opened in the event of

You said that in the event of, you would like instructions straightforward, simple, which, you understand, I've never done.

There is a daylily named Curious. Available (I've prepaid) at Dorothy's Dance Garden. Have one Curious bulb placed in my left hand and two bulbs placed in my right hand, making sure I hold both hands together under my left ear so I can hear the quickening, can think the effort of what is growing through me, feel the three breaking the closed shell of my hands, the shale of my head, naturalizing beyond me, causing me laughter at the comedy of winter failing to kill rot's regenerating impulse to root, to be rooting, to drift in time-shifting twinning and tripling, to signal turning up and leafing before shooting out molten gold blossoms, the moist swellings and retractings and wet collapsings, the retreating from sight, the returning to my head and to my hands, the multiplying, the perennial drama of trying to hold too many, of letting them go, all of them in their cycles of emptying out and lasting too long, so much like me, like me becoming more sod than sot, more site than slot, while they slump, sift, slighten, disintegrate, disappear, lilt, reappear, lift as they feel, think, hear light.

I'll let you know when I've solved the issue of the gravestone inscription.

The problem is, as all problems are, a matter of tense.

Either: *He wasn't always dead.*

Or: *He isn't always dead.*

Or: Blank.

My own dear sons, you're welcome.
                         Your father

On the day I wrote this, spring had come here, and damp cold.
Wind whipped the abundant petals from the cherry blossoms
and sent them whirling with snowfall. For one moment, I
wished to continue living. And for another. And for another.

Blankness is best.

Is it?

A Decade of the Sun

B and his friend Rooks watch the slowly turning head of fire, the way the jets of magma shoot out and collapse in unhinging jaws, in wounds, in singing, singeing mouths. "It's like She has exploding eyes," says Rooks. Says B, "That part! See! She's burning cooler." Rooks never can see the nine hundredth of a second of shift, though the two cindermen have called up this NASA site a dozen times a day in a dozen weeks for months on end in order to sit for the one hour and one minute and eighteen seconds of *A Decade of the Sun*. They are hooked too deeply to unhook.

A year, five years, ten years pass from the time of first viewing. Caught in the single seconds representing days, old men all over the planet are virally affected, and cannot stop sitting before Her, Her full decades-long rotation observable for the first time in film history. They mute the orchestral accompaniment provided. Like all suitors, they constantly adjust and increase Her display brightness. Their photochromic glasses darken. Their mouths cannot close, their throats constrict. Necks, shoulders, backs, hips stiffen.

Rooks crouches closer to Her image as She veils and unveils Her powers.

He moans what he wishes to say. B, his brother in the sunlight ceremony, believes he hears the words, Mother of God. As children, they had accepted stern warnings to never look at Her, and now their eyes are full with the permission they have been given. Pain comes by degrees too subtle for B and Rooks to believe that the torrid viewings are blinding them, year by maculating year. Ten years with no adult supervision, no unspoken prohibitions of civilized, sane society, no eclipsing inner censor.

What do old men do with their lives at the end? They hook up one last burning time. They ask for suffering they have not known. Their mouths full of silence fall open. Ten years after the release, two hundred million men are blind, can't speak, can't move except to turn away from their last-loved and new beloved ones and from spellbound male companions. They turn with Her as She turns. Their hair glistening like mercury, their pupils scorched silver-white, light-raked faces frozen in rictus, they bow more deeply down. On hands and knees they sway, moan in tight circles.

She will say nothing. She has said nothing to them that they can remember now. As far as B and Rooks know, as far as old men ever understand, She will not give back what She gave them: She, the commanding light that grew them and made them fruitful; She, the sun from which they fled. They can't be freed by Her kiss, by Her hair tumbled down from a tower. She will not send them for the slipper that will determine their fate. She will not choose them from all Her ripening, bold choices at The Ball, and transport them in a grand carriage. This is not that tale of terror, the one cinderwomen tell their cinderkind. This one is the story of cindermen kneeling.

(CHILDLAND, Public Library,
Desordenada, North Carolina)

Chapter B, p. 101, *The Ample Book of Alphabetical Puzzles*
by Dr. Crystal Lithium

Buzzle

_ _ _ _	Death by displacement & release.
_ _ _ _ _ _	Death by going & by bringing.
_ _ _ _ _	Death by increase & by decrease.
_ _ _ _ _	Death by learning & by leaving shame.
_ _ _ _ _	Death by displacement & release.

Answers below.

Instant

Rocked gently, trapped facedown, my shroud closed tightly over my waist, I died a little, the ink from the gash in my head spilling. Died more, my mouth sucking in, the curtains of my lungs too oversoaked to draw themselves open.

Died inside a voice calling—"Wake up, water's boiling"—coming from the bumping, exuberant fists of killing current. "Oatmeal's on, I'll eat yours mine both." Died in a tunnel of warning—"Get up, asshole."

Died in a misfitting friendship. You don't think I will?

Died inside a tone shift—"Guess yours'll get cold, we got camp to break steep hike to the falls—this is why no one goes with you—you know that, right?"

My pal flipped my kayak in order to save my life. I couldn't know, but I could tell because the husk of me could tell without knowing. He shouted his own name, "Ti-im! Ti-im!" instead of mine. If his had capsized, we would have died tapping blindly at each other's occupied but quiet shells.

"In there? You!" He was not talking to himself but to the other me. He dragged me to an outcropping midstream, the water making the sound of crystals clicking in a threatening snowstorm.

"Dead," I answered from the husk in which it seemed I wanted to stay, walls flapping, dawnlit wavemouths kissing me. "You prick!" said Time—or Time's pal or Ti-im—splashing us into a better position.

He situated my limbs, turned my head, tipped it up, back, spooked by the doll's-eye reflex of my coma gaze. Terrified and self-terrifying, he screamed, "Ti-im!"

Was that my name? Was that my drowned-man name? And mine had gone?

Something like laughter coughed out of my blue tongue, blue face and throat. *Don't do this. Every morning. I'm sick of oatmeal.* He slapped me, trying to hear laughter again, had he heard laughter, had that been the sound we both heard, two slapped drums thrumming? Had he been laughing but thought he might've heard someone laughing? Without words, I said, *Sick of oatmeal, gimme anything else, anything you bring, I won't complain waitress-campdaddy, cold this morning, pal–cook–ex-friend you crazy fuck, anything but not oatmeal god no.*

He lifted my eyelids so the bowl full of Ti-im came into view. The I in my eyes told him nothing he wanted to hear, the boy compressing his doll's chest, giving his doll his breath, spitting out, screaming at the damn thing lolling in the dead zone, and giving his life, the unliving doll repeating, "Dead," the word some headwater region of my brain spoke. The word gave Ti-im hope since he thought the dead did not speak.

Who told him that? No one. He would have had to imagine.

I did not say but said inside myself quite loudly, *That—booger-stuff—that—kittenshit—that's how perfectly happy campers die who should've stayed asleep.*

"What!" I said suddenly. I coughed up water, annoyed that not another cup or half cup of my lung's misery could come out. "What've you done?" I asked, imagining his stupid savior's sporky, oat-gluey smile.

You ever have a friend who drowned on your watch? Nothing you could do? You did nothing? Was that the right choice? You did something because you thought he asked you something? You think you're the only person inside his doused brain who comes to his mind's dark caves when they're darkening?

"You drowned," he said.

"Slept in."

"No," he said, rough with me, unable to keep me from slumping forward, head lolling. "You drowned. Now what—now what?"

"Drowning," I said. I was. After rescue, I was continuing to drown.

He tried to wipe my dead face from my face, splashed my head and neck, said, "Quit shitting around this is getting old."

He breathed his name into me. *Ti-im*. Not a good taste.

Who was I when the EMTs drained me? I had a name I liked to say because before he melted away, my father had that name. If they failed to empty me, I would die without saying my name, my own name, his, lost in the pool under the falls, in the churn, scooped up, thrown down again, my father, my stone and my river bottom.

When they asked Tim for my name he said "Ti-im!" to them. They asked for a last name. "Ti-im!" he said.

Who rolls the oats—seriously, what kind of job is that job, the job of oat-roller?

Vomiting, I have learned, is the least difficult of the de-drowned undead person's difficulties.

Do you paddle the oats, is that how that works? Wear protective gear because of the deadly oat-dust? Rip-flow-friend-seam, what they were doing hurt like hell. Did I say I wanted to wake up— for that?

The nurses rotated me like a barrel of gefilte funk. Ti-im sat in the hospital room chair for the twelve-hour procedure. He said he sat there like a pat of butter or a piece of toast or a glass of juice. He must have been so hungry, thirsty, wanting to be squarely there but of some use, not such a useless, mute doll caring desperately for his doll. He must have needed rescue from his guilt.

"Hey, pal," said I from behind the rails of myself, from under a buzzing fluorescent moon that was arm's reach from my face. "Hey. Did I ask to spill and seep the rest of my days?"

"Hey, pal," said I, "did you really forget my name when you saved me—hell now, don't weep about it, if you remember then tell me."

They wrung me. *O Time they wrung me!*

Like how you turn a sponge in your fist when you squeeze it dry.

Streams fall from your palms and move in unquiet tongues away from you. Like the nonsense talk of water on flats, on curving depressions, on plunging downspillings, boiling crashings, killing counter-cycloning forces.

Hear that? Hear that? We gotta get there.

Hold. Still.

These two ticks, who crawled from the meadow that you walked across barefoot, docked at your left ankle's pulse-point, and disembarked, and sprinted up your leg.

And paused behind your left knee, and sprinted up your thigh, and toured your soft parts, and motored up your side to your left underarm, and docked there and—

Voyaged your back to your hairline, and slowly bivouacked in a hungering dream through your hair follicles to the summit of your scalp, and stopped, too exhausted to vacuum up the scant blood-dew there, and parted ways and individually descended you and homed in on the places behind your ears, and feasted and swelled.

And swelled. And forgot your body's acclimating camps and the difficult chasms and eerie marshes and smooth paths of you. The two drilled, they drilled, they swelled to the point of outburst, to the point of chording, they strained and strained as they became source and system.

You can no longer displace them as if in some process of editing your skin.

You need our limited and vast expertise.

We press each tick's firm bubble, and we caress and slightly, slightly crush the way one does with all living twin persisting prepositions. We stun the thing with heat of such particularity it causes desiring release. With nibbed tweezers we lift the bit of lusting word-krill and—

Of course.

We place that visitor next to the visitor from your other part, and we observe as one mounts the other in a ritual of climbings-under and climbings-over.

We do enjoy our furious small tasks.

We do.

Now, if we emplace these two ticks again on their human homestead—like this—like this—hold still, please—

—and we wait for only a matter of hours or days, or weeks, we can watch each retrace the original path.

You can feel this breach even if your skin and flesh only mildly attend: the one travelling you.

And—

The two.

Bilateral leukhusanblepharoplasty metemenhancement

Before surgical intervention, Patient's eyes bleb, seep, muddle, trickle, drool: the result of drooping upper eyelids. As ophthalmic mobility deteriorates, perception jumbles, sparkles, molassifies. With progressive prolapse, attitude protrusion undermines impersonal facial features. Through repeated efforts to exercise elevator muscles, unwelcome transcendence rapidly arises from the "bonfires on the beach" effect of inward-looking. If the blepharoptosis persists, intense universal love follows from abnormal unattached focus. Loss of illusion, ascendence of clarity, sacralized sense of impermanence occurs leading to incurable expressive ocular declamations of unconstrained compassion.

Leukhusanblepharoplasty metemenhancement (LMPME) can tighten elevating muscles to infinitesimal degrees of precision. In many successful cases, Patient's supraliminal capacity for proprioceptive visual adjustment can positively result in micro-suppressible basal and reflex lachrymagrandiosis. Surgery can produce absolute control of psychomotor onset of tears in right and left eye: right eye evidences pain first; left eye evidences pain-in-happiness (referred to as "fog light distress-deliverance"). LMPME can assure total cure of all interposing awarenesses. LMPME can result in cure of hoodwink-, fugitive-, foreskin-lid facial appearance.

Outpatient procedure. During recovery period, licensed metemenhanced assistance required to replace bandages in imperturbable darkness of sterile isolation. Note: in rare instances, irreversible baleful-, cavefish-, phoenix-, bisoux-eye may result.

Tartarus

His eyes hooded by drooping eyelids, he wonders if the blue-glass cast of the three-story building is blue.　　　Seems like underside blue or inside-out blue.　　　Seems like the boundless blue from which comes all the sky hues he could perceive before his compromised eyesight reoriented his brain into seeing blood-red thrips feasting upon the world's moist pigments.

In the elevator, Yew shakes herself out before pawing the middle button for Tartarus Surgical. She nudges his left pant pocket because petting him there reduces his anxiety.

She is not a comfort animal, not a trained guide dog.　　Yew is not Master.　　He is not Master.

He thinks of her as the creature who thinks of herself as the burly companion his brain has made to drive with him where he should not be driving, to help him pick humanfoods and delicious crunchy dogfoods from the grocery shelves, to place the blurry items on the conveyor belt, to feel the belt carry him and her through the world's automatic double-openings, to the car lots, the slight and steep hills, shoulders, and side-walk sinkholes.

When he thinks how much he owes Yew for his safety, he wonders how she will regard their partnership post-surgery.

In the Intake, the blepharoplasty metemenhancement patients are greeted by a friendly Intaker in a room filled with companion creatures and their sight-challenged elderly humans. He is asked if he has followed fasting guidelines. Hair, teeth, general hygiene taken care of? Yes. There is a form Yew's man must sign that indicates who will transport him after the procedure. He lies, three times: Yew's last name is also his, it says so on her collar, it does.

He slyly signs the form, nodding his thanks, receiving a no-prob nudge from Yew. The rest has been prearranged by phone: the disclaimer statement, the insurance coverage, medical background information including relevant familial history, allergies, anesthetic responses, psychiatric anomalies; the copy of the living will; the past experiences, if any, of surgery.

The Intaker, Iris or Ares or Eris, a person formed by an almost cohesive swarm of professional manners, asks, "Companion will keep copies of intake materials? Companion will remain in Waiting?"

Yew lightly nose-nudges his belly.

"Yes," he answers the Intaker, his head aching from caffeine withdrawal. "Yes."

"You may be seated until we call you."

He's aware that Yew has heard the first "you" and the second "you." Yew always responds when her name or name-approximate is invoked: the cue is something she does with her forehead, to which he is newly sensitive.

His badly unbalanced chair is not the one toward which Yew guided him. Yew's forbearing smile is his favorite of her smiles:

how much it would mean if he could see that again. There are, of course, greater pleasures in life.

Are there greater pleasures in life?

The two are in the Ring of Waiting under the three giant lamps hanging like clappers inside the domical tetrahedron overhead. The dome's electronic wallpaper fades in and fades out images of a tidal lagoon filling and flooding at silent dusk and darkening the sullen liquid surface and emptying forcefully and emptying utterly at silentest daylight.

Entertaining riddles and postponed answers move clockwise in the chyron under the lagoon projections. The letters are ludicrously giant.

Why is a boxing match like a ballroom?   Why is a night sky like a movie actress? Why is a biscuit like a gardener?   Why is a staircase like a death mask?

Made of flooring.   Starring.   Made of flower.   Staring.

His father had blepharoplasty metemenhancement surgery at about the same age as he. He told his son that much worse things could happen to your features and your outlook, and recalled that his own father, too poor for even essential surgical correction, held up his eyelids with his fingertips when he wanted to see, and when he did not wish to, he remained lidded. Before he could ask how long grandfather was like that, his father said, "Eleven years."

He repeated a phrase his father commonly used: "A round number of years," though he was not sure he had said it aloud. No one under the dome   that is, no one in the lagoon seemed to hear. The most memorable words his father said to him: the most memorable his mother said: the most memorable words from everyone he outlived: with no understanding of why, he brought the words with him to this day. He brought them with him to the Red Paper Lower Level where he was first evaluated. He would bring them with him for his post-surgery evaluation on the Paradise Upper Level. He had the particular words of his father with him now at the Tartarus Ground Floor.

When a person gets old enough to conjecture how long he and his spirit-companion (his sole companion) might live, he rounds down. Or up.

He rounds and rounds.

He schedules a blepharoplasty metemenhancement.

The chyron recycles the riddles and solutions. The lagoon fills with the sighing and resettling sounds of pre-surgery patients and creatures seated under the Ring of Waiting. He and Yew glimpse nothing actual in the resonances of the little crowd's undefined faces.   Some have books they ignore.   Some, hats and purses.

Some dab their eyes with tissues.   Some, with sleeves. With the backs of their bare wrists.

A cloud that looms over the lagoon enshadows this henge, a sound of wavelets pawing the shore, a smell of old humans almost sloughing off their wet old-human bark: in response to it all, Yew glows a deeper aril red.

He feels the glowing of her.

He thinks, at first, he hears a chew-toy exorcise its suffering through brief squeaks.

With greater keenness than ever before, he senses that wait-ing-until and waiting-for are stages of re-forming. Until he met Yew, he was fairly sure he had concluded with the need to answer another and yet another confusing ailment by address-ing them in the order of the most pressing (eyesight, earsight, high blood pressure) to the least (foresight, gum deterioration, hemorrhoids, dyskinesia, crossover toe), to the very least (sca-ley scalp, dysphagia, dyspanegyria, dyspepsia, hindsight).

A tide of night stars jitters in the dome, burnishes Yew's head and back, spreads nebulously through the stove-coil red of her tail.   Yew does not like to be touched. Not any-where.   He knows this, yet the *Oh! But!* of yearning-de-nying comes to him reflexively, and, as ever, the *But... Oh...* of denying-yearning.

Sensing his condition, she touches his right foot with her left paw.

He likes to be touched.   Anywhere is fine with him.

At this particular moment, the signal from Yew is clear: *Don't.* Don't touch back. Don't whimper, "Yew! Yew!" and dry cry in response to my beauty hurting your parched, vexed eyes.

Don't. Don't nervously blubber-laugh and hold your hand over me in some kind of air-pet.

Don't change your mind. Get cut, get the cool eyepatches, the eyedrops, the aftercare instruction, the beacon, the elevator ride. Move on, move on, old human.

 Fixed for irreal minutes in the group's dozing, he says out loud to Yew, "Okay already."

The draining lagoon sounds like the dozing people in its thrall.

Why are bitter lovers like bodily humors?   *Why are false tes-*
timonies like broken church bells?   *Why are full wallets like*
flocks of ducks?

Biles.   Libels.   Bills.

Dr. Koalemos   *Dr. Koalemos*   *Dr. Koalemos*

His surgeon.   His surgeon.   His surgeon.

The Intaker's Assistant touches his shoulder, guides her hand
to his elbow, lifts him, a light and willing man now, an unac-
cented word, the middle number that is one less than the next
number though one more than the previous.

As he is taken away, he hears seabirds singing somewhere
in the shifting sky above and, impossibly, behind him. Two.
Two.   Two.

He hears a little Do-this-Get-er-done grumble. "Bye, Yew,"
he says.

Yew lifts her head, feeling that she is almost rising into the
chyron.

Does he matter to Yew?   He matters.   Why does he
matter?

Why is a comb-over like a hangover?   *Why is a jumping frog*
like an alcoholic?

Why is cremation day like payday?   *Why is a climbing plant*
like a penalty?

Dogged by the hair that bit you.   *Distilled.*   *Urnings.*
Vine.

*   *   *

Swoony is how he feels post-surgery, seated again in the lagoon, Yew at his side. The Assistant has put into his hands a device the size of a deck of cards. "Your beacon," he is told, "indicates when you can go. Your post-op appointment is tomorrow morning: Paradise Upper Level."

Yew is pleased that he is pleased with himself. Yew smells the fear-sweat on him, the off-gassing of doubt. The human goo, seepage, drool.

Seems the inflow and outflow of the lagoon is one hour of ticking sound.   Seems the appearing and reappearing cycle of the chyron is one hour.   The traffic in the Ring of Waiting drains down and fills in the temporally predictable pattern of fairy tales.

The beacon shivers to life, the circle of red beads shines. Reading his thoughts, Yew opens her mouth to carry the alarm away.

Yew

Two days after the surgery returned his sight to him, Lagan asked Yew, "You want to go to church today?"

Her answer was yes—yes, of course. But she did not bark yes at all like a churchgoer. In their time together, neither of them entered the broad white doors of Mary the Dawn Catholic Church, though they walked together every day along the wall of the churchyard.

In the days when he lived without Yew's company, the crumbling brick cap of the wall had provided Lagan with a guide during the critical period that his collapsed eyelids had at last degenerated to the point of leaving him almost blind. In the two-acre churchyard he could rest his right hand there, at shoulder height, and walk until he returned to his starting place at the churchyard gate, a one-hour journey when he strode fast and, strangely, a one-hour journey no matter his pace. According to the season, the churchyard's mercy-light had trembled in particular sections of the curved wall and had warmed his forearms, neck and shoulders, his eyelids.

He felt soothed by the scraping sound his palm made, the sound of spreading salt over a cutting board.

When she had joined him at the gate one evening and walked by his side for the whole walk, he asked, "You from around here?"

The creature had appeared as if from tree shade. He thought she would surely leave when he left.

He asked, "You Catholic?"

He told her he had been raised Catholic for a round number of years, but that was seven decades ago.

He wanted to know, had she ever sung "Mary the Dawn, Christ the perfect day, Mary the gate, Christ the heav'nly way"?

Walking together, they did not collide, though colliding had more or less become his habit. A good mirroring rhythm came to Yew and him, a four-legged and two-legged groove of locomotion.

She had simply picked up Lagan, a stray in the churchyard.

"I liked that song. A beautiful song." He almost sang the words; instead, he said, "Your tail is red as a flame azalea, even I can see that," and reached down to touch the place he thought her head might be.

She growled, *Don't touch.*

"Me," he said, "I like to touch. Like to be touched. You can brush—see there, that's what I mean—you can brush yourself against me. Don't trip me up though, I'll wander off and then—who knows?"

No answer came. "Who knows?" he said.

No answer.

Had he imagined this walking companion? If he had not, why the silent treatment?

He had talked too much, that was it. He lifted his hand from the wall. He fearfully put it back and brushed his palm twice over the surface, which whoosh-kissed like tumbling beach sand. He *did* talk overmuch: the price of long periods of solitude was that his self-talk escaped: he didn't have to be told that he tolled and tolled like an alarm bell in an empty school.

"You there?" he asked.

A goldenness brushed the wall. "You," he said, tears pouring from his broken curtains and down his face. The ring his life was fitted to—the habits inside the ring—he heard no congregation singing there, though he could retrieve a few phrases of music; he felt he could not walk the miles and miles of Time to meet the singers, to hear the whole hymn lifting them into another condition.

Her friendly growl, coming from deep within her, reached so far inside him the locked-away word, *miracle*, came and, of course, spilled out: "You're a miracle."

His companion barked. Her bark-phrase was exactly in his own tone: Okay, already.

He named her Yew. They were, after all, in the company of the churchyard trees, some over seven hundred years old, guarding the graves with faces rubbed clean, their features worn down to riddle letters and riddle spaces. In some of the yews, small creatures rustled, resettled. In some of the yews, the heartwood, hollow for three hundred years, drummed sympathetically to percussion in their own roots and the roots of others: Whom. Whom. Whom.

He had known Yew for three weeks before the day of the surgery. She stayed with him. She cared for him. Without her, he knew he would have cancelled the procedure and never rescheduled.

* * *

Three days after the surgery, when Lagan was free of the eye-patches, he and Yew walked close to the wall.

Lagan said, "Remember the lagoon?"

Yew coughed quietly but agitatedly. The lagoon. The chyron. The Intaker, a thin creature wearing socklettes that left the appealing marrow of her hocks exposed. So hard to look away from the skin barely covering the bone.

"Remember the place?"

Of course.

"Me neither," he said.

Lagan floated his hand over the crumbling cap of the wall but did not touch. He looked like humans look with one wing tucked and the other flying. A human-like that would roam a parking lot, one hand on a cart, and be all right. A human-like that would suffer less in the abyss of any new ailment of the present and ache of the past. A human-like that would delight more than ever at being touched by other humans. Lagan—healed up good, for now—was in readiness to leave the first of the rings of waiting, and the next and next.

At a particular place in their circular journey, Yew always paused. A good place to smell the air, the ground, to crouch and relieve herself.

Lagan, an old human, liked this rest. Time curved here, and here he found dark peace with his losses.

A small female, more toddler than pygmy, fell out of one of the trees and landed directly in front of them.

This surprised Yew not at all. Calmly, she left Lagan's side.

The jumper held before her a yew-spear tipped with a merlin beak formed from aluminum foil. She hovered the spear tip over Yew's eyes: each eye.

"Miss you," she said.

Yew pushed her whole face into the blue sweatshirt over the little person's belly, turned her head to the left and to the right, pressed more deeply into that sky. Seemed like the water-bowl blue of a clear day. Seemed like the pulsing blue that birds suppose they alone possess.

"And you are?" asked Lagan.

Ignoring his question, she said, "I was here—up there—when Em chose you. She never did that before. Never. Saw you, chose you—"

Now he understood completely, now he understood not at all. "How?"

"Went off with you. I was eating the red berries I never ate before. They looked good. Em said, 'Don't, please, poison, please don't.' I did though. Then Em, well, she couldn't make me not eat.

"She doesn't beg. Ever.

"She stood under the tree.

"She stayed.

"Well.

"Well, after Em went with you, I fell out. When I fell out of the tree, I went right in. Into the dark where I could eat all the everything I wanted."

She touched her wand to Ems's tail.

Lagan said, "She doesn't like to be—"

But Em did.

Em liked to be touched by the magic in the little person's hand. Lagan saw her hand so clearly. He saw Em's whole body reach up to receive the spell of the red-stained palm, of the small, pale fingers.

He heard the trees drum the way they drum in fairytales to call us from this side of our wall to the other.

And the child and Em went away.

And they have never been seen again.

Prose poem at sunrise

When he retired from the steel mill, B's dad, a WWII veteran, played golf at an Army depot golf course. He was there two mornings every week, joined by other old mill friends. In the club's Mess, a burger, beer, and fries cost you a $5 contribution to the VFW. The Mess was the home of a painting entitled, *1st hole—sunrise*. The title had been painted onto the molding, which was the size of a small barracks window and was sticky to the touch. B saw the thing many times when he caddied for him or picked him up there. B's sister, the youngest, who knew their father best in his old age, observed him closest. She said he would forget that he had asked her if she had ever seen anything like the thing, and he would insist she look again.

At the same tee depicted in the thing, B's father had a massive heart attack. The version of his death B heard is that he fell to his knees, got up. Fell. Came to as if in the haze of a seizure. During the speeding drive, the ambulance attendant, a parish friend, asked him about his handicap. "Hay fever—hay fever's about it, I guess" was his answer.

He loved that thing, the smeary dark version of a mist-smothered dawn. The fairways and greens were mostly painted in black too thickly applied, the trees full of neon-blue–black leaves and the bleak sky resenting the sun.

Is it raining or about to rain in the painting? Is it fall or spring or summer? Is the country going out to or coming back from war? You can stare for hours and only wildly speculate.

There was probably a concentrating, bent-over veteran lining up a putt on one of the greens beyond the 1st hole green. There was probably a golf ball or bullet or comet flying out of frame at the upper right corner, and someone on a distant tee trying to follow the trajectory. Wasn't there oily smoke coming from the Mess exhaust or, only a few miles away, the gigantic smokestacks of the steel mill, or, further distant in time, the rain of exploding earth and mud?

There was probably a bicycle or a starving dog leaning against a fairway fence. Or a statue set on its side. Or a groundskeeper napping. The badly painted inscrutable figure in that part of the painting might have been a shadow falling into the thing from outside the margins.

A porkpie-wearing man adjusted his grip in the rough; a wolf-ish boy loped behind him; behind and a little above the boy was the boy's thought-whorl (or canvas flaw), a simulacrum of the porkpie man in a wadded form.

Trained in painting and writing but doing both terribly for the past five decades, B recognized that the painting, an almost-ness of a high and very low order, was not a shapely piece of art. Friends knew that his dad loved the prosaic thing because he said so: "The thing has character," he would say, which was his highest compliment. He felt that to lose your character was to lose your perfect imperfectness: to build character, you did many regrettable things for the right reasons, including choosing the wrong profession or faith, keeping the peace with the wrong friends or family members or your own wrong nation. Soldiers who were braver than others but would not follow unjust orders had character, he said. He told

B once, "No one knows the truth about Sacco and Vanzetti, no one ever will—but I tell you, their story had more character than everyone else's."

The artist brought the painting to the funeral service, explaining he had to steal it from the clubhouse in order to bring it. The two men had, as the painter put it, "kinda served together." Service members and work friends were there for B's father, as he had been there for them. A dozen or more perfect flower arrangements surrounded the thing, which was on a flimsy homemade easel at the foot of the coffin.

B's sister and he could not agree who would have the thing. "I'm the youngest of us five," she said, making her claim as illogically as she could. "I'm the middle child," B said in order to answer absurdity with absurdity.

Calculating, correctly, that B would cave, she kept the painting. His sister, who could not survive her decades of alcoholism, died at fifty-two. B understood that she had more character than he would ever have even if he should survive his own choices.

For a time, no one knew where the painting was, though his sister's husband thought she might have taken the thing, as usual, to her last rehab center—through many rehab attempts, too many to count, she always propped the thing up where she could look. When she and B would talk on the phone, often the conversation degenerated into differing opinions about the weather there—in the painting—about the sunrise—she said, "sun*set*"—about the trees—topped—"no, *pruned*," she said—about that dog or bicycle or whatever that was leaning against the fence—about the river flowing through the soot-sky—"a symbol," she said.

B has the painting now. Though the thing has none of the most-all-ness you might think a thing should have, something like the thing's almostness is what B would offer were he ever to write a tribute to his sister and father, were he ever to offer a thing they would value in the way they valued this thing, made by a painter with a low opinion of the sky, of the land, of the place of dying.

De-installation ceremony, Whitherton, North Carolina, May 18, 2019

The old man asked, as our truck strained against Time's weight, "What've you done to their little hands? What've you done— what've you done? This here isn't right, and you know it," and he said, "We mightn't've minded if you'd took him and his wife and daughters down with more respect for their station."

We had chained General Bragg's ankles and the ankles of his four beloveds, and had manacled their necks and wrists, and pulled burlap hoods down over their heads. The job took us all morning, so, coffee breaks, too many. Had to piss on their bronze backs and legs, on the mother's flowing gown and on her daughters' gowns, a sheen of gold streaming down the gold-green hems.

Imagine the sculptor's concern for conveying the free motion of those grand five striding reconstructed into the future, rock- ing back and farther forward, bowing solemnly, then a deeper falling before their screeching crash onto our truck bed, down from the high pedestal of their century after unimaginable loss of family pride, of rank, of tribe, of empire.

"How much're you making for this—can't be much, can it?" He kneeled down to our bound captives, raised his fist, not a fighting fist but the kind that couldn't let go of bloody dollars and coins and the oldest, bloodiest bills of sale in our rural town.

"This," he said, "is history, our history,"

and ran his hand over Eliza Bragg's fine walking dress, the romantic, stylized embroidery design of shagbark hickory and the dense knotweed veiling our Georgia woodlands where Chickamauga Creek flows into the Tennessee River. He touched the artist's embossed brand on Eliza's nape.

"You don't understand, you can't destroy this."

When we already had, why say we could? In fact, we'd made some income, not as much as transporting pigs or chickens or cows, but more than you'd think we would. Our operation didn't make the television news because no parading brown-shirt Proud Boys came, and the daughters of the daughters of the Daughters of the Confederacy stayed home and read to their children, and because the president, whose mother never once put a book in his golden tiny hands, was golfing at his resort in Mar-a-Lagos.

But we did get mentioned by the local radio commentator telling how effectively we conveyed our goods for shipment to their distant destination, giving us more or less an advertisement for our business. The commentator reported that we had "cruelly" taken the little bells from the children, describing how we had knocked them out of their claws with single, hard hammer strikes and, then, smashed in the fingers.

As everyone raised here knows,

those handbells were a problem for the whole one hundred and twenty-three years since the monument first claimed the square. The sculptor had fitted but not affixed them to the children, and, as a result of that poor planning, sooner or later some Whithertonian souvenir hunter would take them. New bells were manufactured using the original molds. They were quietly replaced, though always soldered wrong to the hands.

Over time, they would be stolen again.

This had happened on at least six occasions, often enough that a line item went into the town budget, and police here doubled their vigilance, and thieves their strategies.

And a man, a proud, hardworking family man and Confederate descendant, had made the monument his mission and point of exchange after he had lost his sobriety, his home, church, and family. He had, he said, already lost his country.

He had, he said, already lost his country.

We picnicked in the truck in order to hear the whole story from him, an outcast even in this, the town of his birth, the county of his ancestors.

We shared our lunches and sodas with him. He was one of us, by which I mean familiar-strange.

We gave him the loose change in the truck's cigarette tray, explaining that we had got it from the Major General Polk Memorial in Raleigh, North Carolina, where folks considered it good luck to push coins in the major general's open mouth-slot.

Where would we take them, he wanted to know.

"The Good Place," we said.

What could we say? Scrap heap. Eternal fire. Mass grave.

"What more can we do for you?" we asked.

We fulfilled his request, simple enough.

We removed the hoods, though not the restraints, on the Bragg family members.

We let him touch Eliza a final time.

He fondled the jacket over her dress, the capes and bonnets of the children, the children's happy faces, their torqued shoulders, arms, wrists, and the jagged places where their hands had been.

We let him touch

Eliza's unwrinkled brow, her crushed nose, her open smile, her manacled, wrenched chin and neck.

A week later when we returned to tear down the pedestal, all six square feet of brick was gone. In only one week a new sculpture—must've been in the town's backlog of monument storage—had been installed: four larger-than-life but lifelike bronze pigs rooting in a pool of darker bronze. The shining, permanent slop featured the inscribed words, "Where's Papa going with that ax?"

Mollycrawbottom

Dear Chief,

Thank you for acknowledging that all your senses, all your heart, all your mind comes alive in response to the small, badass, bucket-eye creature of mine you have rejected—pugnacious-looking mollycrawbottom (no larger than your wet thumb or your cauliflower ear, no smaller than your dry prick), partnered in a dance with the algae-stained river stones upon which it licks at tasty flecks formed by slip-streaming sunlight, while enclouding itself in Paleozoic silt by circular tail-flicking and fin-flexing, shuffling promenades shaming mere ballets of swimming. I should not have sent it to your publication, that small hospice aquarium.

In the currents above mollycrawbottom, the speeding traffic of hatchery rainbows muscles old, untamed Appalachian browns to exit lanes and into streams and under crumbling cutbanks on poison-crusted agricorporate land. Still, in the collapsed arteries of the watershed, the mesmerizing, calming beings creep-swim. River guides call them "bad first drafts of baitfish," and field biologists say they are "easily mistaken for rifle shells or discarded triple-A batteries." Before the age of reason, every child draws this same womb-fresh swimmer from dream-memory, pooling and riffling and releasing world in one body with vague margins. You have had no niece, nephew, no children, grand or great, no childhood, then?

You with your fine-mesh, small-net heart, with your search engine replacing your instincts, with your neck stiff from self-sniffing, what species do you assume will outlast the most recently dismissed? What species will endure despite you?

I am sorry to learn that you do not believe readers would find this underworld aliveness enough.

I will now wander again into the woods where rustling dead saplings, despoiled rank nests, bitter-tasting fruits—where singing-flying seeds drumming fragrant rains & & & fantastical frog hordes rough-lusting in puddles—are "all too complicated for a sufficient number of readers to relate to."

Respectfully,
The Author

Birder

"Oh, for a trap, a trap, a trap!"

Let's be clear. I'm the birder here.

You are not.

This walk we will take into the sonic realm will, at times, seem unreliable. And that is because.

Because the art of birding is, like all art, an unsolvable crisis of beauty, a galaxaphone in a cave with distorting echoes coming from and traveling in all directions. Sound's refractive characteristics share almost everything in common with memory. In the effort to retrieve memories, you hear yourself misremembering.

Was your mentor's name Pea? Impossible.

Was your father, a serious mental case, named Case? Really?

Trying to recall a single crystal, you produce the blinding crystal forest hiding that one memory. And I, expert in identification, am there—and, also, here—trying to make things better, Children, but.

Good question. You are not: Children. And I: not. But you are my Children for now. And I your guide-child.

Good question. We will not encounter bathrooms or bath-rooming possibilities at any point, I'm afraid. Return to the parking lot now if you have pressing business.

Go.

No. We will not wait for you, and I absolutely do not encourage you to catch up with our party.

The blazes on this particular trail do not mark locations accurately since the weather and the beetle conditions here wipe them.

Should you become lost, walk forward—not back. A forest surrounded by forest surrounded by wilderness is not a place to return from. You move in. The portal you did not expect and do not want expects and wants you.

I'll explain.

There are beetles, they say, who can only reproduce when female and male eat blaze paint and suddenly find each other terribly attractive. Until that time, they are beetles living in domestic stasis, more or less as they expected.

There is a name for them. Yes, I am dressed in their colors, red and yellow, darker red under my piebald coat collar. See?

What is their name? I admire them so.

What is their name?

They make a sound—three shrill notes—that imitates the radiating, dissolving sounds of the Smoke Wrens who are their mortal enemies.

Do not follow any sign that indicates falls ahead or loop trail or lookout or ridge trail or primitive campground or rim route or ruins or historic ruins. (Any hand-carved sign that says "BS Trail" means what it says.)

I'm afraid walking forward is the only way. At daytime: forward. At night: forward. Acceptance. Abiding. Abiding acceptance is the key, Children, since there is no singular Rescue Rule for leaving fantastic lostness: you are at least as old as I, and, so, you understand that bitter, beautiful truth.

The beetles are called.

They make three shrill notes, maddening, like the squeak-shrieking of rats. I can't think of what they are called.

Are you lagging already? Rouse up!

Put your hands up if you're a lagger.

Won't admit it? What, I ask, is worse than a liar-lagger? What, I ask—

That sound there!

That sound is two quickly disappearing sounds intersecting. The song comes from two creatures of the air under the high canopy of those Crane Oaks—see them there? Well, imagine them—imagine the oaks are named that because from an omniscient view they appear as two legs joined at the conjoined canopy that is their giant green body floating, swimming with other green bodies in mountain mist suppressing rising music, churning and mixing and thickening and thinning and atomizing sound and noise.

Trail markers of OU do mean. Something. They mean Origin Unknown. Let me know if you see one. A good sign.

We do not need to walk quickly in order to hear, to begin hearing millipedal phrases grooving the air, moving slowly near, to begin imagine-remembering phrases not there now, not there ever. When my brother, Ricky, disappeared here, he was a grown man who had followed coupling beetles somewhere to a place he called "Out of Reception."

He's hereabouts.

Ricky is here. He comes into and out of Reception and every few years he phones to tell me he's okay, still leases basement space in a bear den, but won't give me a findable location. Says that once in a great while he sees Pea, who lived here and was a kind of adoptive graymother to us two all-but-homeless Curran brothers. She called herself Mayoress of the mounds of green that hid her from view in these woods. Ricky says when he and Pea meet up they make pie, eat shrooms together, drink a trepanning potion, freak out, vomit in her tiny fireplace, rebuild and retune the tiny fire tongues, repotion, refreak, reshroom, repie, reintroduce themselves, repeat.

And when they talk about me, they cancel out the truth of my true self with contradicting memories of how and who I was.

That's what Ricky says.

Hey, Ricky!

Hey! You home?

Haven't heard hair nor hide of him. Too, too long now. And the killing virus has traveled from city street to city park to the parkways and onto pathways, from tree body to tree root to leaf, from fresh blaze to wiped, from orgiastic beetles in wet heat to beetle-eating songbirds high in their snug, rumpled nests—to vulnerable human hermits quieted by living apart from the din of humans' unceasing, spreading noise.

You had family members and near-friends and far-friends killed during Chapter One of the killing Covid-time? Raise your hands.

Of course. Lots of you.

Did Chapter Two kill more? Almost kill you? Chew on you, suck something out and bring to life some new aberrant anti-brain in you to fight off new invasions of resilient thought?

Put your hands down. I didn't ask for a show of hands. This isn't a game of Simon Says.

Put your hands up if you feel you are now or ever might have been a carrier.

Put your hands down if you went maskless and definitely killed someone.

And Chapter Three?

Put your hands up if you are an unashamed super-spreader—

down if triple-vaccinated—up if double—down if ashamed

—up if the guilt is making you sick—sicker than you've been your whole life—

down if the guilt is killing you—way down if not

—way up, way, way, way up if not at all, not one bit.

Oh, they were delicious edible beetles, any bird could tell you that. They wore the turquoise of pool-cue tips. That foil-blue shimmering on fabulous dragonfly tails. The sea glass eyes of augury dolls.

Hey, Ricky! What's that beetle named, Brother?

Is Pea dead?

Jesus. I wish you'd answer. Answer yes or no.

Are you dead? Is Pea dead, too?

Okay. Answer with a branch shake. With a stomp. A declarative fart will do.

I still think nothing could kill her.

But—you. I still think everything could kill you, Ricky.

"Chad," you'd say to me when we were hiding from Case, "don't let him kill me. He could do it. He could do it too fast for you to stop him."

"You'd have to stop him all by yourself," I always said.

He was quick, our dad.

"You'd have to stop him all by yourself," I always said.

Neither of us believed you could.

Our dad was able to be not this and not that. The law would get him, then not be sure what they'd got. A "notty" is what they call a deadly, natural-born vermin like him in these parts.

I'll never see Ricky again.

Will I?

I thought it often when we were little. That Case would kill him. That I would have to kill Case. And keep the secret. That I would have to kill myself or my own children to kill my ghosts and have some peace.

How many of you will come right up to the familiar swale of under-memory and sub-thought where someone you've lost lived. But?

But will not come out again?

You, too? Raise your hands.

Higher.

Liar-laggers.

We are a group exclusively unyoung! That has never happened in all my many birder tours over the years! I'm glad! You're glad, too? Isn't it good to have the common bond of loving the dead nearby, among us, as indifferent to us as if, in the forest of our feathered bird surfaces and inner organs, they reside as reproducing, consuming syllables of gnawing life?

MST and AT mean Moon-Sap Toast and Ant Tits. Signs of danger.

We have not gone far in, yet have gone too far on some side trails unrelated to our main trail. This is one of those moments when you might think, Is this birder a false birder? Or you think, Why do I—did I—need to know the names of the birds? Some of you know the names, some of you learned them as children, and suddenly you doubt yourself. Some of you convinced yourselves that outside—in Nature—you were safe—

—and sound.

Have you only just met the person you are at this moment? Out in Nature, do you ever feel you've come under the bad influence of your own worst nature?

Oh, Children. Oh,

Oh, listen! Seamstress Hawk!

Let's sit on this couch of grass—oddly depressed, isn't it?— where we can hear the hunting bird ripping the fabric of morning.

I have a bit of pretend tea I've brought that helps with terror.

I've brought a pretend infuser and tea-muslin and origami napkins and—sit, sit—I've taken delicate cups and saucers straight from favorite storybooks—here, this is such a good place to unbox and unwrap our tea service. And to set ourselves down almost between the FUU and FUL stakes, which very definitely mean Fuck U Up and Fuck U Up Loop. No arrows on them. So. They mean YAH! You Are Here!

Sit.

Sit.

Put yourself atop the earth that will top you. Lie back. Lie back into the feeling that you never can go back.

One day I lost most of my hair here. Fell off. Away—

—in one violent gust.

If you find some, please—you must—gather the hair up for me.

Nut-brown was the color.

In case of fear, I've got a pretend teapot with pretend sweat on the browning surface. Isn't it a wonder that pots are thrown and saucers fly and tea goes in you and then leaves?

In case of darkness, I've got a candle-lantern and a referee whistle and, in the instance of attack, real invisibility havoc-hats.

We're one hat short, by my count.

Best not to dwell on that.

Let's settle in. We've one cup extra. We've plenty of sparkling sugar cubes like no cubes any greedy, hungry child has ever sucked down to nothing. We've miniscule spoons with sharpened handles. We've the feeling we can rest our old selves once and for all, listen for the one sound.

I remember the name of the beetles now!

No.

No.

I'm not telling.

Listen, my dying Children. You can hear them coming.

(Print, *Head of a Bear* by Leonardo da Vinci, ca: 1480
exhibited with note of warning in Public Library,
Desordenada, North Carolina)

DO NOT TOUCH!

If art falls you could be injured

Blue Squill

Grateful for his body's productiveness, Mr. Jordan Jabbok took three satisfying morning walks in order to piss a circle around his newly planted blue squill bulbs encircling last season's blue squill plants orbiting his weeping cherry tree sending its large but tender roots under a ring of curved red bricks, reddish-golden now, and fringed by high blue larkspur rising from within a circle of squill planted in other seasons, and smelling like strong rat poison when they are in bloom.

The long, masterful piss on a daily basis was the expressive performance of the retired ballroom dance instructor.

"This is how you begin?" my restless sister asks. Adept at mocking biblical jargon, she says life permits two choices: "You can ask, 'Why *is it so?*', or you can say, 'It is so.'"

Certain tales answer the former question.

Certain tales, much smaller, embody the latter. This one is of that kind.

Mr. Jabbok's bladder was in peak condition from two years of battle with the crows enjoying their own dancing in his plot. If you asked, he explained—bragged, really—that his impressive piss volume had grown with the help of maximum hydration, blood pressure medicine, beets in his morning shakes, bad dreams and long griefs needing discharging, and, of course, intense bladder-release focus.

He reminded you that he had not picked the fight. He was making a refuge for the struggling and the surpassing forms of beauty humans attempt to foster while on their knees in their imperfect gardens. He was making a refuge that he must defend.

The crows, at first, took only his bulbs out, ripping them from their hiding places the moment their first roots dug down to taste deeper, fertile darkness. Mr. Jabbok put the bitten ones back in, replaced the others like a man rewarding thieves by bringing them fresh candy in samplers.

In the next season, the crows, who could imagine blossoming enigmas far beyond God's imagining, bit off the tender green fingertips of his plants that the crows had located precisely in space and time. They repruned emerging shoots so that everywhere in the garden were angry, suppurating pimples of dispossession. Any plant that releafed in response to pruning so enraged the crows that they slowly tugged the plant out whole as a worm and juiced the thing—root tip, root ball and green hat—in their bills, and guzzled down, and guffawed. They spit the garden's promises in oozy arcs under which they pirouetted on flexed talon tips.

"They have a story that overwhelms Mr. J's story," my sister says, who always has an opinion about what a storyteller like me should understand. I call her my demented mentor. She calls me Mr. Lit.

I keep the peace with her. I ask, "Why *is it so?*"

My sister never answers or even begins to answer something she believes she has answered. She should move out. I should tell her she is ready to stop living with me when she starts her new job. She has left before—many times. She should leave again. She eternally starts a new job, distinguishes herself as the hardest working and best-loved employee, loses the job, starts another. Seeing this pattern from the outside, you would think you are seeing the whole pattern.

Mr. Jabbok had heard that bears and deer and squirrels and possums and rabbits and even snakes could not tolerate human urine. It turns out, wise-sounding amateur naturalists, that the urine humans make is a godlike substance that is the deliquescence of poisons the human body remits in undiluted streams. It hisses and steams and voluptuously glistens and sings as the spellbinding rank scent of healthy human approaches you. If that acid wand touches you, the merest splash leaves a cursemark from which you will never be released.

The crows were, at first, convinced.

The wisest among them explained that Hell warns, "Here demons swim," when comes the sound of unzipping. The crows wept in pathetic shrieks at Mr. Jabbok's piss giving them instruction in the human Frame, the Basic, and the Progression over the garden's Lines of Dance.

Mr. Jabbok thought there was no bird more beautiful than the crow when black rage blackened it, when indignation deepened the bird's velvety blue hue. He could stand in his pissy garden and plant seeds and bulbs and seedlings, and whistle-sing, "Prettybird*pretty*BIRD*pretty*!" and see with his own eyes how their busy, well-groomed heads lolled from agitated boredom.

He understood that the god of Eden had given the crows a thirty-million-year head start in understanding how to sow retribution. He was unsurprised when they stole his paper from his porch and confettied the news over his place of retreat from the world. He was unsurprised when they dive-bombed the outermost parts of his garden with the shitbags from their nests, defining in no time at all a slick dark corona difficult for a pisser to cross.

They captured other smaller birds and bled them in bright sprays over the battlefield. They tucked one carcass inside another to show him their understanding of repulsive-re-splendent design.

They changed the codes of call and the codes of song to make themselves untranslatable to him. They revised the codicils in their contract with the resident hawk, and, as a result, torn-apart, half-alive rabbits and mice crawled over the garden carnage.

The hawk threw down also the head and the feet of a young crow: a sacrifice he apparently required in the negotiations. He crashed the headless torso onto the porch in place of Mr. Jabbok's news.

The crows brought tools from their hiding places: shards of glass that would cut Mr. Jabbok's feet, shiny square shaving blades that would shiv his face, hooks they carved, fins they contrived into serrated knives. They complicated perfectly his stuck-in-the-craw bad situation by quieting absolutely every songbird and singing bug in the woods.

Mr. Jabbok, who understood nature's unalterable cyclic forces better than most, knew the jury perched all around him would not adjourn. He had only turned to the piss cure when he could think of nothing else, he explained again to us—that is, to his loyal troops standing or squatting as we must to join him in his cause.

I signed on because—why not: the whole routine of my too-long life in the yearlong days is after-breakfast writing and coffee-drinking and pissing and all-day writing with more black coffee at hand, and after-dinner writing, and writing with beer assistance but more or less writing piss before quitting late and leaving my pages every night with no sense of their use.

My sister, who did not join us, who says it is best that she should be unnamed in this tale, agrees with me that I was a perfect fit for the crusade, like a chain-smoker wearing a suit of smoke.

My sister has opinions. "Quit philosophizing." "Quit decorating." "Quit reading Poe!" she demands, by which she means I should read her Poe-lite hero, Stephen King.

Mr. Jabbok had seemed nonplussed when I first walked the hundred yards out of our woods and waved to him, and, without further greeting, entrained myself to his singular task. The human duty of guarding a green being has nothing to do with who asks, who answers.

It is so.

Is it so?

We do not live unless we are planted, do not give to the earth until we are given.

Aren't you writing a story everyone reads when you respond to the inescapable pressure and unzip and spray as we do: in a design that contention and communion have defined. Aren't you? The weeping cherry tree casting petals, the squill and the larkspur and cosmos, the prolific black-eyed Susans, even the butterflies and bees and wasps and ants and the tree frogs in the hardwoods surrounding me and the old pisser and our troops—all smell like piss and crow shit.

The crows smell like bulb spoilation and human urine. If you listen closely, you hear them calling out the same thing as the old pisser when they fly down, dig, eat, leave, return.

Amen is what they're saying.

I joined the dance there in that one place calling to me because my writing life had made me a devastated and undeterred gardener-gladiator. I stood under the storm in a state of wonder.

I witnessed in Mr. Jabbok's militarized garden the yellow rain and yellow snow the shade of that marvelous Penn tennis ball color called ITF Yellow. I understood the color.

Sixty-nine years ago, when I was teaching my sister to walk—I was the ten-year-old designated babysitter—she somehow associated holding a tennis ball with walking. If I gave her the ball, she would stand, start walking, holding it slightly before her, gazing self-hypnotically at that yellow sphere marked with the pale white moebius stripe. She would throw it down—stop walking—make me fetch—walk.

For an inappropriately long time, she would not walk for anyone without her companion, whom we named ITF, of course.

Her walking with her magic friend: those days gave me such laughing-out-loud joy. At all points when I remember that period in her life and ours, greater joy arrives, and it has broken open more room in me for welcoming the magic hour and the magic object held forth as a projection of holy possibility in a world that has lost all sense of the sublime.

I was not at all surprised to find myself—a piss-poor bread-winner, a piss-rich example of a grown human—a warrior in a piss war.

As a writer, I've recognized that more gold appears in sunsets now. Last pulses of light branch and bear red-gold leaves that tremble as they fall. Over nearby cities, the fog that doesn't quickly lift spreads dirty lightbulb-gold dust over parked cars, over dog walkers and their dogs, children and their school backpacks.

I've prayed on the kneelers I've made out of sentence-flotsam I ripped from poorly constructed sentence-boats rowed by gods alone with their gods. All christs of all kinds and religions, I've learned, are piss-christs. The nimbus of language they swim in lifts them toward a heaven smelling like all things tortured, crucified, buried, resurrected glorious. I've learned that stories should end by adding something that will result in a sense of honest fullness. I've learned that stories should end by subtracting something that will result in a sense of honest emptiness. I've lost the gist of how stories should begin.

Mr. Jabbok's story ends as you would expect

I believe I will eventually write a story with my sister as the central figure. She reads my few published works, knows them well, likes to remind me that she reads more books and bigger books by far than I, likes telling me her ideas for what needs to be written that no one seems to write.

Her proposed narratives consistently include her own story of winning self-understanding. She has convinced me—during this, her fifth post-AA period—that if your entire adult life is claimed by addiction, addiction looks to everyone you know (mostly addicts—are you convinced you are not one?) like the story of your life. Every day of her failing efforts against her addiction, she insists, has given her more insight into her weaknesses and strengths, her last and first assumptions. I think that is true. I'm not sure, but I think it is so.

There is something weirdly right, she says, about the fact that she will never kick and stay kicked. That "success story" would, after all, mean losing her way. And there is something right in the fact that no one but her can recognize her real story. And there is something wrong in the fact that she could deliver Mr. Lit her story, and I could want to write about anything else ever.

I have tried so hard to not write her story, to not let it over-whelm the other stories I have in mind or have underway. Now that she has become permanently resident in my life and now that I'm old enough I can die and can be certain that my meager offerings as a writer die with me, I should feel free to write her story, shouldn't I?

It is so.

But. Dear Sister.

Dear Sister, *is it so?*

Do you see that holding your story before me leads me nowhere? Do you see that holding your story before me is the only way I can gaze into the world and stagger crazily around in the failing gardens?

Mr. Jabbok's story ended as you would expect. New human friends enriched his life to the end. He lost the final battles in his war with the crows, and he lost the war, and what remained when he died were his neighbors, his loyal piss-companions who saw to it that his ashes were spread as he wished, where he wished.

"Make a truce," were his final benevolent words. He had spo-ken from deep in his bed, and was hard to understand.

Perhaps he had said, "Take a piss."

I have told my sister about the brief evening wake ceremony in Mr. Jabbok's wrecked, quiet garden. I have reassured her we will both be fine if she stays longer, though I know she has already taken that for granted.

I have described for her how shapes lumbered, shivered, swayed out of the ground and came through the woods and toward us during the ceremony—opalescing fog devils that the wind spun out of the groundcover spume and the creeping air.

"That's how you end a story?" she asked, as she always asks.

(Rain song stenciled on the crown
of the cupola above The Reading Room,
Public Library, Desordenada, North Carolina)

Do *dee*
do de do dee—

do *dee*
do de do *dee*—

"How to bear happiness?" Number 81 in line asked DMV Clerk Number 7, who requested vehicle registration and referred the matter to Clerk Number 9, who did not swivel as many clerks feel they must in swivel chairs adjusted to great heights with height adjustment levers, and said, "This one goes upstairs," and conveyed the questioner up several narrower and narrower flights and past numberless corridors of echoless peace, though not of exact silence, of matters gliding onto inboxes and lifted newborn from outboxes, of piquant complaints and compliances, and, faintly, the nerveless laughter from shuffling papers, then up more flights, steeply up, at last into The Office of The Clerk of Happiness who called out, "Next, please," the Clerk's hair at the temples marked by cream cheese icing or streaked in an icing effect, not a superior official, yet not extraneous, who smiled a you-may-leave-now smile at Clerk Number 9, indicated a not-too-distant seating place into which 81 could be seated, took the small tongue-shaped paper proof-of-number into hand, sat down, petted the 8, petted the 1, petted, stroked, straightened in posture, seemed to chew or in secret to say something kind, to notice for the first time the moonscape lint illuminated on the resin schoolroom desk of quarter-moon design, a clerk desk inappropriately small for the cavernous dark room, no doubt a room within a grander, darker room, petted, stroked, petted, licked the dry 8, licked the 1, pressed the paper number tongue down onto the desk surface in an attempt to lift the gathered-together subtly scented exoskeletal spirits up for inspection, pressed one last time, punched the satiated tongue onto a spike of tongue-hundreds at the desk's outer edge, and followed with a searching gaze the stirring atmosphere of the desk edge, the desk's outer atmospheric forces sweeping out beyond the edge, and gazed at the room's walls, at the grand-room's and great-grand-room's walls, at the solemn rotations of down-drafting office fans or primitive ferns or inchoate clouds overhead, at the faint lint throngs skating in conditions of felicity upon the office floor tiles, teal blue terrazzo, and gazed at the language reversed on the stenciled opaque glass of the office door through which 81 had entered, and The Clerk of

Happiness touched a fingertip to the spike tip, pressed down but did not pierce the flesh, lifted, pressed again, seemed to be sensing death's seams straining or perhaps life's or perhaps the lifting up of and lifting off of all assumption or designation, and from inside The Office, a universe of brightening pellucid ice, The Clerk answered:

Number 81, what you thought is not true not true not true not true not true: you thought that your beloved could annihilate you or would if you created a space in you no larger than an alms bowl, and asked, "What is the sin in us living in joy together?"

How to go?

Go the way you came.

Next, please.

NOTES

A decade of the sun

July, 2020, in honor of the ten-year anniversary of its satellite, the Solar Dynamic Observatory, NASA released a time-lapse of the sun's last decade. You may wish to observe this one-hour video (in which each second corresponds to about one day on Earth) set to a custom soundtrack by musician Lars Leonhard here: HTTPS://WWW.YOUTUBE.COM/WATCH?V=Y_Q_IG9C46S

Circulation

Mark 9:49 (KJB): "Where their worm dieth not, and the fire is not quenched."

Buzzle

Answers: Born Breath Bloom Blame Borne

Birder

The epigraph "Oh, for a trap, a trap, a trap!" is from Robert Browning's "The Pied Piper of Hamelin."

Rain Song

When asked how he conceived his solo "Singin' in the Rain" dance sequence, Gene Kelly said that it was "all in that little vamp, do *dee* do de do dee—do *dee* do de do *dee*."

ACKNOWLEDGEMENTS

A Literary Guide to Southern Appalachia, Eds. Rose McLarney, Laura-Gray Street, University of Georgia Press, "Mollycrawbottom."

Cincinnati Review, November 2022, "Six Portraits": "A difficulty," "If a small ocean," "On the 6:25 a.m. Tunnel Rd E1–427," "Wineglass," "A wish," "Oak."

Crossing the Rift: North Carolina Poets on 9/11 & Its Aftermath, "Let us draw near," (reprinted from *Scoundrel Time*), September 2021, eds. Joseph Bathanti, David Potorti, Press 53, NC, 2021.

The Glacier, January 2023, "Prose poem at sunrise" (previously titled "Thing").

The Georgia Review, Summer 2021, "De-installation ceremony, Whitherton, North Carolina, May 18, 2019," "'This,' he said, 'is history, our history,'" "As everyone raised here knows," "He had, he said, already lost his country," "We let him touch."

Permafrost, March, 2023, "Instant."

Ran Off with the Star Bassoon, December 2022, "Parable of the Robe."

The Rupture, June, 2022, "Blue Squill."

Scoundrel Time, September 2020, "Let us draw near," "Checklist sharpied on the inside lid of a hatbox," "Sharpied on a damaged MAGA car windshield."

Superstition Review, Winter, 2021, "In the garden."

West Branch, March 2023, "Tartarus" and "Yew" (titled "Tartartus" in that publication).

Kevin McIlvoy has published six novels, *A Waltz* (Lynx House Press), *The Fifth Station* (Algonquin Books of Chapel Hill; paperback, Collier/Macmillan), *Little Peg* (Atheneum/ Macmillan; paperback, Harper Perennial), Hyssop (TriQuarterly Books; paperback, Avon), *At the Gate of All Wonder* (Tupelo Press), and *One Kind Favor* (WTAW Press); a short story collection, *The Complete History of New Mexico* (Graywolf Press); and a collection of prose poems and short fictions, *57 Octaves Below Middle C* (Four Way Books). His short fiction has appeared in *Harper's, Southern Review, Ploughshares, Missouri Review,* and other literary magazines. His short short stories, poems, and prose poems have appeared in *Scoundrel Time, The Collagist, Pif, Kenyon Review Online, The Cincinnati Review, The Georgia Review, Prime Number, r.k.v.r.y, Willow Springs, Waxwing,* and numerous other literary magazines. He received a National Endowment for the Arts Fellowship in fiction. For twenty-seven years he was fiction editor and editor in chief of the national literary magazine, *Puerto del Sol.* He taught in the Warren Wilson MFA Program in Creative

Writing from 1987 to 2019; he taught as a Regents Professor of Creative Writing in the New Mexico State University MFA Program from 1981 to 2008. He served as a fiction faculty member at national conferences, including the Ropewalk Writing Conference (Indiana), the Rising Stars Writing Conference (Arizona State University), the Writers at Work Conference (Utah), and the Bread Loaf Writing Conference (Vermont). He was a manuscript consultant for University of Nevada Press, University of Arizona Press, University of New Mexico Press, Indiana State University Press, University of Missouri Press, and other publishers. From 2017-2020 he served as a fiction editor for Orison Books. He served on the Board of Directors of the Council of Literary Magazines and Presses and the Association of Writers and Writing Programs. He died September 30, 2022.

About WTAW Press

WTAW Press is a 501(c)(3) nonprofit publisher devoted to discovering and publishing enduring literary works of prose. WTAW publishes and champions a carefully curated list of titles across a range of genres (literary fiction, creative non-fiction, and prose that falls somewhere in between), subject matter, and perspectives. WTAW welcomes submissions from writers of all backgrounds and aims to support authors throughout their careers.

WTAW Press has instituted an annual book prize to honor Kevin McIlvoy. The Kevin Mc McIlvoy Book Prize will open for submissions in 2023, from which a distinguished panel of judges will select a manuscript of prose for publication. The winning manuscript will receive a cash award and a standard book contract with royalties.

As a nonprofit literary press, WTAW depends on the support of donors. We are grateful for the assistance we receive from organizations, foundations, and individuals. WTAW Press especially wishes to thank the following individuals for their sustained support.

Nancy Allen, Lauren Alwan, Robert Ayers, Andrea Barrett, Mary Bonina, Vanessa Bramlett, Harriet Chessman, Melissa Cistaro, Mari Coates, Kathleen Collison, Martha Conway, Michael Croft, Janet S. Crossen, R. Cathay Daniels, Ed Davis, Walt Doll, DB Finnegan, Joan Frank, Helen Fremont, Nancy Garruba, Michelle Georga, Ellen Geohegan, Anne Germanacos and the Germanacos Foundation, Rebecca Godwin, Stephanie Graham, Catherine Grossman, Teresa Burns Gunther, Annie Guthrie, Katie Hafner, Christine

Hale, Jo Haraf, Adrianne Harun, Lillian Howan, Yang Huang, Joanna Kalbus, Caroline Kim-Brown, Scott Landers, Ksenija Lakovic, Evan Lavender-Smith, Jeffrey Leong, The Litt Family Foundation, Margot Livesey, Karen Llagas, Nancy Ludmerer, Kevin McIlvoy, Jean Mansen, Sebastian Matthews, Grace Dane Mazur, Kate Milliken, Barbara Moss, Scott Nadelson, Betty Joyce Nash, Miriam Ormae-Jarmer, Cynthia Phoel, John Philipp, Lee Prusik, Gail Reitano, Joan Silber, Charles Smith, Michael C. Smith, Marian Szczepanski, Kendra Tanacea, Karen Terrey, Renee Thompson, Pete Turchi, Genanne Walsh, Judy Walz, Tracy Winn, Rebecca Winterer, Heather Young, Rolf Yngve, Olga Zilberbourg,

To find out more about our mission and publishing program, or to make a donation, please visit WTAWPRESS.ORG.

WTAW Press provides discounts and auxiliary materials and services for readers. Ebooks are available for purchase at our website book shop. Readers' guides are available for free download from our website. We offer special discounts for all orders of five or more books of one title.

Instructors may request examination copies of books they wish to consider for classroom use. If a school's bookstore has already placed an order for a title, a free desk copy is also available. Please use department letterhead when requesting free books.

Author appearances, virtual or in-person, can often be arranged for book groups, classroom visits, symposia, book fairs, or other educational, literary, or book events.

Visit WTAWPRESS.ORG for more information.

WTAW Press
PO Box 2825
Santa Rosa, CA 95405
WTAW@WTAWPRESS.ORG

Other titles available in print and ebook from WTAW Press

Promiscuous Ruins by Julian Mithra

Eggs in Purgatory by Genanne Walsh

Mississippi River Museum Keith Pilapil Lesmeister

One Kind Favor: A Novel by Kevin McIlvoy

The Groundhog Forever: A Novel by Henry Hoke

Like Water and Other Stories by Olga Zilberbourg

Chimerica: A Novel by Anita Felicelli

Hungry Ghost Theater: A Novel by Sarah Stone

Unnatural Habitats and Other Stories by Angela Mitchel

And There Was Evening and There Was Morning: A Memoir by Mike Smith

The Truth About Me: Stories by Louise Marburg

Printed in the USA
CPSIA information can be obtained
at www.ICGtesting.com
JSHW020809190923
48241JS00013B/20

9 781733 661935